I0685614

A MATTER OF ORACLES

Kaye Boesme

Aigletos Press

2023

eBook ISBN 9781735740652

Print ISBN 9781735740669

This book was published by the author under Aigletos Press.

Contact information is available at kayeboesme.com

Cover art © 2024 Lori Williams, licensed for use by Kaye Boesme for the distribution of *A Matter of Oracles*. The artist's contact information is available at graytiger.net

୫

To the Mistress of the House of Books,
You of the Cord and Rope,
Who Rejoices in the Chamber of Dark Ink.

୫

CHAPTER ONE

Tilōno could date the moment she decided to become a librarian to when she was nine. It was ten days after midsummer in Owá, Demza, years before her initiation into womanhood, when she used the simple pronoun *le*, as all children on Atara do before initiation.

The family had lived in Demza since spring, and Tilōno still spent ler mornings commuting to the catchup school two train stops away to learn Demaí. Ordinary school instruction would happen in both Demaí and Classical Atarahi. Until the immigrants mastered it, there would be no studying in school with people ler age.

Being nine and sitting each day for so long filled the young Tilōno with a boiling restlessness, and that restlessness served as the linchpin — years later, le could identify how the move and adjusting to a new culture brought lim to learn what le could contribute to society, and le even used the story during ler librarian apprenticeship interviews. That summer was etched in ler memory because it had had good helpings of both happiness and pain, of curiosity sparked and curiosity rewarded.

School concluded just after noon, when Tilōno, ler six-year-old cousin Vūwong, and the other Demaí students filed into the lunchroom to take their food and eat under the flat-leaved courtyard trees. They cleaned their plates, tidied the school, and took the train back home together. It was the Purple Line, and the development they lived in was still new. At the edge of Owá, it housed mainly other Midway immigrants like them, but nobody Tilōno's age. There were plenty of young kids like Vūwong, brazen and oblivious.

Owá homes were not hospitable to Midway culture. They had no natural dividers to separate men from women, so Tilōno's older relatives had added their own — a curtain that ran down the center of the living room. It was from the store and still too short, the extra fabric waiting for a robot to sew it up once it had some time, so Tilōno could see the men's feet from the women's side and vice-versa. As children, Tilōno and Vūwong could move between the men's and women's spaces, as could Sōno, the only sselē in their family who had moved to Owá. Sōno had never cared for the rituals of men or women.

Owá was landlocked, at the convergence of two rivers, and far from the ocean. Maqá, the capital city along the coast, was about four hundred kilometers to the south. Midway was equatorial, and Owá high-parallel. Demzang homes had large, open living rooms on their first floors with cozy nooks and small bedrooms for family members on the upper floors, the spaces heating-conscious and claustrophobic. The two conjugal visit rooms had a separate entryway along the house's side, near the kitchen. Tilōno missed the old house on Midway Island, its tropical trees pregnant with fruit and protected from vermin in the two separate courtyards, boats lowing in the distance like herd animals.

Demzang summer days lasted long into the night, hour after hour of daylight, a jar overflowing. It was hard to sleep when sunglow poured through the cracks between the sunshades. Verb conjugation tables danced in ler head when le closed ler eyes. Restlessness fluttered in ler chest and stomach like a caged bird.

Tilōno often took to sitting at the window late at night as the sun set, listening to the sounds of crepuscular and nocturnal animals as they awakened and to Vūwong's steady breathing. Le let the shade up just enough to peek out.

Their childhood window faced the only old thing in the neighborhood.

It was a wall so ancient that Tilōno fancied it had stood since the early days of Atara's colonization. Beyond it lay well-kept prairie and distant buildings overgrown with plants like something out of a fairytale. The ground cover continued as far as le could see up the hill beyond them. When le squinted, le could barely make out an on-demand rail track, too rusted and ill-used to glint in the light.

Automatic robots trimmed and neatened the property, usually at night, but never touched those buildings. Tilōno watched them unfailingly.

Le had never seen a person enter or exit those buildings. A bit morbidly, Tilōno wondered in the beginning if the property's owner had died without a soul noticing, the robots left on their programming cycles for all eternity. Those thoughts ended one night when a trimmer broke down. It wasn't there when le awoke.

That morning, Tilōno left the house after washing and before breakfast. Le walked up to the wall and took a good look at it. Trees grew against both sides, trivially easy to climb. They could hold ler weight and had low branches.

It was three days after midsummer. Tilōno wasn't wearing anything that stained easily, just a school uniform, so le checked the branches. Some wobbled, but most held lim steady. Le found a perch and looked over.

The other side's fields were filled with fleeting, sky-hued summer flowers. Tall ūdo plants rustled in the wind, and a robot moved through the fields thinning everything out, making up for what had not been done the previous night.

At nine, Tilōno was not naïve enough to climb the wall and trust a trimmer robot to detect a living obstacle in its path. Le climbed back down the tree and jumped onto the ground. The wall could wait until the next day when the robots were back on schedule.

It rained for the next three.

Tilōno spent most of ler time studying for Demaí exams in VR. The AI customized the difficulty level just enough to keep Tilōno tired and frustrated. The garden level was the worst. Tilōno didn't even know the Classical Atarahi words for all of the plants in Demza, let alone their Demaí equivalents, and now le had to name all of them and all of the local idioms in which the plants' names appeared.

It was this exam that finally pushed Tilōno over the wall. Le wouldn't have a grade for several days because it had an essay portion, but the lessons had turned to crumbling mica underneath ler stylus. Demaí was allegedly similar to Classical Atarahi and the Midway language Tarmei, but Tilōno had grown skeptical. How could they truly be part of the same family when Demaí was infatuated with forest metaphors, but Tarmei loved the sea?

The weather had been good long enough for the trees and wall to dry out. The robots wouldn't do their evening routine for at least the next two hours, and there was only a small colony of mēs grazing through the trimmings. Tilōno was tired enough of the newness around lim to hope for something better and older — houses that had stood for hundreds of years, the foods of home, really anything — that the wall *did* become that thing from fairytales, ripe and waiting, ready to pull the child forward into a world beyond anything le could imagine. As le climbed, le counted to ten in Demaí. As le moved over the wall, le narrated. Everything came fluidly. It had just been ler nerves during that exam.

Tilōno scuffed ler right arm coming down from the tree on the other side. The flesh remained torn and static for a moment before blood beaded up on ler black skin. Le wiped it off on some leaves and decided to take care of it later. Nothing was broken.

Some of the flowers had bloomed after the cutting, but not all. The remnants of their bright petals caught in the crevices of the waist-high ūdo. Le picked one of them and put it in ler hair.

It took more time than le'd planned to trek uphill to the buildings. They'd only been a distant vision from Tilōno's home. Up close like this, the complex of buildings — menageries — was massive. It appeared to be a scientific breeding program, still with signs of people. The old light rail system Tilōno had seen from the window led on towards more buildings, an estate house and some smaller structures in the far distance. The property must have stretched for kilometers on ler left.

Most of the buildings were locked. Tilōno tried each of the doors, listening first for the sound of any adult who might be working. Something inside made a flute-like call from low to high and back again, like an opera singer, answered by many more calls. Some of the notes contained clicks and deep-throated trills.

They sounded like hāyiko, *haíko* in Demaí, but these noises were far less threatening than the carnivorous animals. Tilōno tried to peer through one of the windows and glimpsed only a smear of movement. The animals inside lived in open enclosures.

The final building contained no high-voiced animal noises, and it was unlocked. Tilōno slipped the door open and peered into the murky darkness.

There *were* things that looked like hāyiko asleep with toys, food bowls, boxes, and perching shelves, separated from the remainder of the room by a perforated glass wall. They were three-quarters the size of a grown hāyiko, with iridescent, purple-on-night-on-green down covering their beautiful bodies. One of the animals opened a single set of eyes drowsily, its other two sets closed. The blunt beak remained shut. The sensory spines on the animal's face were half the length they should have been.

Another awakened, and it bounded down from atop a cushioned box and right up to the glass. Tilōno could have poked ler fingers through to touch it, but didn't. It cooed and whined like a small child at first. Then, it opened its beak and sang, eerie and flute-like.

Tilōno would have to ignore it for now.

Le turned around to face the remainder of the room.

This is the moment that le remembered when le filled out ler application for library school at sixteen, the words flowing from ler fingertips like water as le composed the essay. In the semidarkness, ler eyes traced the boundaries between the enormous stacks of paper, most dusty, some not — many lain out in bookshelves haphazardly, some on the floor — and the old-fashioned, chipped computing table with a screen that blinked DATA ERROR like a strobe light.

There were books, too, and data disks so old that Tilōno doubted they could fit in the streamlined players that had been used around the world for the past two centuries. A few modern external drives — the kinds sent in shipments around the world ever since the final oceanic cable's failure — sat perched on a black-screened box that looked like a dead computing table on its side, about two or three times the size of a tablet screen.

It was an overwhelming mess of information.

Tilōno didn't hear the heavy footsteps or the doorknob turning. Le stood frozen beneath the mental weight of the silent pages and disk drives in front of lim until a voice shouted, "*Ćanwé!*" — *hey you*, pejorative sense.

Ler entire body electrified. Le turned around and stumbled back against the damaged computing table. The screen responded to ler touch with a high-pitched whine.

The person staring Tilōno down dressed like a man, but ler face was completely naked beneath the sunglasses — no piercings, tattoos, or paints to indicate gender and status. Ler stomach writhed. Even sselētna wouldn't walk outside with a bare face. It was too childlike — and uninitiated teenagers wore at least plain studs. Le had pale skin and a pointed nose like most people in Owá. Le was short — only a head or two taller than Tilōno.

"I'm sorry!" Tilōno yelled in Classical Atarahi. "The door was unlocked!"

The adult scowled and shook ler head. Le breathed out through ler teeth. "What's your name? Whose child are you, and how did you get in here?"

"Tilōno ō Vōwusī. I live in Creekside Place, in the development over the wall. And — the wall." Le lifted ler hand from the computing table. It stopped whining. "Who are you, and how do I address you?"

"Tekīya. A man." He removed his sunglasses. His thin, narrow eyes definitely marked him as a Northerner, yet not from Owá itself. The irises were bright red.

Tilōno gasped. "You're a haribān." *Aribá* in Demaí.

"Of course I am. You're in the research fields of our estate in Owá. There are signs at the two main entrances. The main house is four and a half kilometers farther into the property. How did you get in here?" Tekīya said. He shook his head. "You sound and look like a Midway kid."

Tilōno shook ler head. "Nobody put a sign on the wall where I am."

"We don't plan on little kids coming onto the property to play," Tekīya grumbled. He closed the distance between the two of them and unplugged the broken table from the wall forcefully.

"I'm nine."

"I'm over six hundred."

Tilōno frowned. It was common knowledge that a haribān was demimortal, perhaps even immortal if the Goddesses of fate wove eternity in someone's favor. "Your place is a mess. Did anyone ever teach you how to clean?" Le avoided calling Tekīya grumpy. "And you're face-naked."

"The animal pens are clean."

"My mom taught me not to be messy when I was five." Le squeezed ler eyes shut and stuck out ler tongue to diffuse the tension. Arguing with a haribān was unlucky. They also ran the medical school where two of ler aunts now worked. "I'm the oldest child in the house."

Tekīya pursed his lips together and threw the unplugged cord onto the ground.

Tilōno turned back towards the documents. Le lifted some of them close to ler face. Written in the men's script, Tilōno couldn't read them, but the handwriting was neat and practiced. "These are all of your records from, like, centuries, aren't they?" Le tested the edge of one sheet. It crumbled under ler fingertips. Even if le couldn't read it, this was more interesting than verb conjugation tables.

"Yes."

"About the animals?" Le peered farther into the darkness. All of the pages le could see bore the same handwriting. It was *only* Tekīya who worked here.

"Scientific notebooks, observations, genetic data." Tekīya's scowl deepened. "I'm making history here. It's not kid stuff."

Tilōno set the pages back down and turned to face the adult. Despite the fear, le maintained eye contact — notwithstanding that ler mother would tell lim to run, that proximity to one of the haribātna could never end well for a mortal child. "Do you need help?"

"No."

"Your face is naked, *and* you're a liar."

Tekīya shook his head. "I told you: I don't want some child playing with my things."

Tilōno turned away from him. Le set down the pages. The immensity of these archives called to lim seductively, embedded in the writing that le could not understand. It was the song of the Reed Goddesses, loud and melodious in Tilōno's ears, entering ler nostrils through the scent of the aging paper — and it was far more interesting than anything le had ever encountered. "Six hundred years, right? Have you been doing this all that time?"

"No, maybe a hundred years, hundred and fifty. It's easy to make tame animals, but—*fuck,* kiddo!"

Tilōno stepped over half-fallen boxes into the papers, holding ler arms out for balance. Someone had overturned the bookshelf deliberately a long time ago, judging from the dust. Le turned around. "I can go to the library tomorrow and see how to take care of this, maybe make the paper stop breaking. Can I? Please?"

Le moved deeper. A box filled with data tapes cascaded to the ground when le touched it, and its contents spilled everywhere

— on old notebooks, derelict tablets, and a hāyiko skeleton that looked too smooth to be real. Tilōno yelped, but tried not to look too scared.

Tekīya followed lim in. When he reached Tilōno, he grabbed ler wrists. The two of them were very close. Tekīya did have piercings, all empty, some half-closed. Tilōno met his eyes and did not look away.

It didn't matter what the haribān said. The unkempt archive had already asked for help. Tilōno would keep coming back, day after day, until cranky Tekīya stopped complaining.

In those late years of childhood, le would learn two important things: Not all things can be digitized, and not everything digital could be salvaged. The world of data disks and virtual storage offered convenience, but its records were as permanent as smoke rising on the Reed Goddesses' altars during their sacred festivals. Paper meant preservation, and the best paper of all was *nābimī*, claypaper, because even fire only made it stronger.

CHAPTER TWO

On a rainy autumn day nine years later, Tilōno processed into the Owá Library's initiation chambers with thirteen of ler peers. They still dressed like students, but within those chambers, Tilōno received the ornately-carved lobe and forehead piercings that marked lim as a librarian who had placed in the top five percent across Demza.

An apprentice appointment came a day later when a robot arrived with an official letter from Maqá. It gave lim a slim fabric scroll and left immediately, flying off through the sheets of rain that beat heavily against the ground.

Tilōno had applied for reference services, hoping to leverage ler stamina in the data stream. The document, in the old-fashioned writing system still used by scholar-initiates, did not say what le expected.

The appointment was to go to Maqá. Le would be stationed at the National Library's Hall of Oracles.

Tilōno knew nothing about oracles.

Le shut the front door and rolled up the fabric. Tilōno wasn't sure how le felt quite yet. Ler hope had been to work in the Wildlife Library just a city away. The more le thought about it, the more viscerally wrong the appointment felt. It wasn't like the movies, where scholars received appointments and paraded around the house with their new scrolls overjoyed.

Apprenticeship appointments came from the government, and unless it truly did not work, Tilōno had to say yes.

It would have been easy to go upstairs and cry — or scream into a pillow — but someone would see lim. Instead, Tilōno unrolled the appointment paper in the men's lounge, again in the women's, and received the blessings of ler relatives. Sōno was busy at the back of the house in the kitchen, and le approached lim last. The deferential smile Tilōno wore when le raised the fabric to ler forehead in thanks each time hid what was, at first, disappointment — and then anger.

Le would break down crying if le saw Tekīya. Tekīya was an asshole about tears. Instead, le sent a message and took the train across town.

Training to take on the responsibilities of womanhood was very different from professional initiation. The idea of being in a community of women excited lim — to follow the Mysteries of Nourishment and the Calendar of Grace, to know the Mud Dance, and to understand the women's writing system. This initiation would last far longer than ler career: The piercings and tattoos of womanhood would follow lim to ler grave. In the final phase before initiation, le couldn't let difficult emotions get in the way of ler performance. Otherwise, le would have to do everything all over again in a new city, juggling the preparations for initiation against the obligations of ler first government job.

One day turned into another. Le didn't read the appointment

message for at least a week. Maqá National Library processed ler paperwork through the Network anyway, and le first read ler job responsibilities there. It relaxed lim to see that le'd still have half-days immersed in the data stream. Tilōno didn't want ler endurance to tank.

Tilōno's womanhood initiation happened in a much larger room than the one for librarianship, among three hundred other girls, conducted by eighteen Mothers of various ages. Tilōno read the sacred texts and made the sacrifices that all people on the verge of womanhood make. Le saw the secrets that must not be revealed, those which gave lim the rights to *she*.

She was bound in each verb and in each emphatic pronoun choice of *gotomis* instead of *tzimis*. Tilōno updated her Registry profile first.

As a scholar, Tilōno could use *ēta*, too — *Ussēta* in its most formal application, both a title and a pronoun. *She* felt intangible, as untouchable as the galactic arm obscuring faraway stars, in comparison to *ēta*'s stately poise.

Tilōno settled on, *Tilōnoki ūtamset i ēta. Amiyaslēf īk Owáqan. I am Scholar Tilōno. Librarian apprentice from Owá.*

Two new people had viewed her registry profile, a person in Maqá and someone else whom she recognized, but couldn't remember from where. It was another woman, the gender piercings fresh and puffy, the chin tattoo's curved lines slick with oil and angry. She was fat in the cheeks and very beautiful. Tilōno blushed. There was also a message from Tekīya, five days old, unread. Guilt led her to avoid opening it.

She was still thinking about the unread message two days later, when she took her last meal in the family's Owáng house. Mid-autumn snow swirled outside. The family performed a ceremony at the door for her, a farewell offering of sweetened alcohol and delicate, ćas-infused bonbons for the household Gods and the tutelaries that had talismaned her since childhood. The bonbons stuck to Tilōno's teeth.

Outside, the dawning sky bled the pink-amber of sea-pearls. The rolling suitcase followed her down the snowy streets, stuttering slightly as it evaded piles of plowed snow. The sun peeked over the trees just as she reached the Purple Line train. The automatic suitcase whirred and came to a stop in the train car beside her seat.

Almost everyone stared down at something — books, glowing tablets, or the small geometric logic puzzles popular in Demza. A woman checked her piercings in a mirror. The temperature would drop farther below freezing over the day, and everyone but Tilōno wore their heaviest autumn coats. Most had switched to winter earrings.

Tilōno leaned back against the glass and stared up at the wall marquee, its community announcements rotating endlessly. Maqá's autumns did not turn cold and snowy so fast, and its skies did not oscillate quite as extremely between all-day and all-night. Her mother had given her clothing for each of its seasons and sub-seasons. Tilōno had two sets of librarian's robes, a new set of scholar's robes, and three student's robes for various seasons that could be sold off to people in Maqá so she could buy more appropriate clothing. She had already connected with someone to trade one of them for a formal Midway outfit.

The Purple Line swelled with people as it came close to downtown. Tilōno detrained at the Owá Central Rail Station. People all around her rushed to work, interspersed with androids, utility robots, and hummod security. She made her way through them to the eighteenth platform, where a messy boarding queue had already formed. Some travelers clustered in groups, luggage pushed just outside of the line, while others sat on their suitcases. Tilōno moved her suitcase aside for a hummod sselē whose eyes glowed, hair-mods scanning Tilōno and the others as le passed by to get in line behind her. Cybernetic body modifications were expensive without plausible justification. Being a hummod meant that someone was wealthy, an important person, in a religious sect her family didn't like, or in a specialized security force. The officers in the Planetary Coordination Authority were rarely that ostentatious.

The line started snaking. Tilōno had to pee, but didn't want to give up her place. First come, first serve seating meant that the people in the first third of the line would have their pick, and everyone else would have to settle for what was left over.

A young woman stopped in front of a station android and half-shouted, *I missed my train*, in fast Demaí. She seemed barely older than Tilōno, with her long black hair fastened away from her face in a ladder braid. She was fat, with most of her weight in her thighs, calves, and belly, and her pale arms bore swirling tattoos from one of the noble families. Her gender piercings were as fresh as Tilōno's, and the tattoo on her chin seemed swollen under the bio-sealant.

Her coat lay over her first suitcase, one sleeve dragging slightly underneath the left wheel. The second suitcase had a placard that blinked FRAGILE. The android took her over to a kiosk, and the young woman started crying.

Tilōno stared at her for a long time before recognizing her profile from the Registry.

"That's an ō Ćedīsam," someone said behind her.

The hair at the nape of Tilōno's neck stood on end. Tekīya. She turned towards him, smiled, and nearly tripped over her luggage as she hugged him.

He was a head shorter than her now that she'd grown up, ever the same.

"You said that just because I'm from Midway." Tilōno rolled

her eyes. She hadn't recognized the noble house markings, but Tekīya couldn't read her mind. She wasn't in the haribānōqi mental collective. She squeezed Tekīya close. "What are you doing here?"

Tekīya shook his head and chuckled. "Someone told me that your train was leaving. You never bothered to visit."

"I'm sorry." Tilōno slipped out of the hug and looked down. A covered box lay beside Tekīya, rustling slightly. It wasn't like him to bring hāyiko to train stations. "Things got stressful."

He rolled his eyes. "I come to this station for your sendoff and find you checking out some noblewoman. Meanwhile, my life has disintegrated into haphazard filing again."

She shook her head. "I doubt that."

"But it *could*." He pursed his lips together and jutted his chin towards Tilōno's luggage. "I listened to the Toast to Our Elders from your initiation on the Owá Professional Academy's audio portal."

"Did you?"

"I can't believe you called me your greatest inspiration." He giggled and pushed stray wisps of hair away from his face. "Luosa contacted me from Maqá and asked if I was ready to take life seriously."

"What did you say?"

"I take life seriously." He rolled his eyes. "That's all paraphrasing, obviously."

Tilōno glanced towards the front of the line, where a utility robot had started taking identity scans to ensure that people matched their reservations. "You've always helped me."

Tekīya's lips curled back into a snicker. He looked at the ground and back up at Tilōno. She'd had enough experience reading him by now to know that he was flattered, not angry. Tekīya said, "And I still can't find half of the things in my collection."

"That's you, not me. They were probably on the shitty dead hard drives."

"Hey." Tekīya's gaze scanned from the front of the line to Tilōno. "We don't have much time before you board, and I have things to say."

Tilōno nodded. The line now stretched around the pillars at the center of the station atrium. It seemed as if the entire city had family boarding this train. "Okay?"

He shrugged off a backpack and opened the drawstrings. Inside was a box. "It took me some persuasion to get this for you. The haribānōqi leadership doesn't precisely see the value of an unproven, eighteen-year-old librarian." He pursed his lips together. "But I have something for you that's intangible, too. Your ID card. I loaded a ten-trip into it so you could visit me in Owá on the express."

The highest-speed train took just under two hours to travel between the cities. Tilōno had booked her travel today on the local train, which did the same journey in just under three. Her brow furrowed. "What are you giving me, Tekīya?"

"That. Um, and something else. I — I want you to take one with you, um, to help it get to know people." He cleared his throat and jutted his chin down towards the rustling box.

Tilōno nodded. Tekīya had been working on indigenous species' genetics for a long time and had data running back to when space travel still existed. Some of his software dated to just after the ship-grounding, and it still expected network cable to run between continents, but the war's cable-shredding robots had ruined that.

He smiled sheepishly, and his eyes tracked the shifts and turns of Tilōno's facial expression. She smoothed her brow into optimism. "It doesn't bite?"

"Savāzi frightened that other one, and this one's nicer." He knelt down and pulled back the fabric over the cage. Inside was a small, domesticated hāyiko, its coat iridescent and fine. "Socialize it."

Tilōno stared down at the box. It was too much all at once. She almost argued that she couldn't feed it, but she knew hāyiko well. They ate small meat animals and flying things, which they grabbed out of the air with their auxiliary, rope-like arms. This one, like all of the captive hāyiko, had stunted auxiliary arms, but they still meandered through the air to sense out prey, complementing sensory spikes on ler face.

"What?" she offered.

"I will have someone waiting for you in Maqá. I don't expect you to prepare the home for it on your own," he said softly. "And you'll have to visit me with lim."

Lim, she thought. "Does le have a name?"

"Āyiki 7," Tekīya said.

"You're using the pet name I gave them?"

"Yeah." Tekīya smiled widely. "They're all āyiki."

She moved forward in line, and the suitcase followed her. "And what if le does something?"

Tekīya put his hands behind his back and shifted the backpack on his shoulders. "Maqá is not so far away."

That is exactly what my parents said when we left, and then the sea's final data cables failed right after we arrived here, Tilōno thought. They still hadn't been repaired or replaced. At least Maqá didn't require intercontinental travel.

"Maqá is not so far away," Tilōno repeated. She stared hesitantly down at the carrying case for the animal. *Pet* was a word she'd learned from Tekīya. Her new housemates would need to learn it, too. "Thank you for the passes, friend."

Tekīya grinned widely. "Thank you."

She gave him another hug. The package pressed into her shoulder, its edges pokey. Tekīya smelled like shampoo, fragrant oil, and the incense offered to the Goddess of the beyond-city wilderness.

Her eyes welled with tears. Each moment from her childhood felt like a movie playing back simultaneously, ready to fall like dominoes. She could not see the future behind her.

The librarian initiatory text said that the Goddesses of libraries, Sanwū and Sasnē, gave gifts to their beloveds, the information-keepers, cultural guardians, and memory-builders of society. If Tilōno had to ask for gifts, she could not have wished for better than the life she had already led. Her appointment in Maqá made no sense, but it had to be good for her.

She slipped out of the hug and wiped tears from her face. Tekīya's eyes were bright, shining. This was hard for both of them.

Tekīya picked up Āyiki 7's crate. He carried it for her until the end of the line. They remained silent, cocooned in the anxieties and hopes of their friendship. He saw her off with a kiss on each cheek. She handed her luggage to a helper robot and went onward with her cabin possessions and the animal, now crying in ler cage. She stroked one of the tendrils to calm lim down.

The robots tossed her suitcase into the baggage compartment as if her entire life weighed nothing. When she boarded the train, she collapsed into a seat as far from the toilets as she could go, just in front of a young couple who'd already started dozing off.

She pulled her knees to her chest in the seat and opened her tablet. A flat documentary stared back up at her, paused on a scholar gesturing at a map of Atara. Tilōno wasn't in the mood for historical drama, especially now that she was leaving Owá. The map just reminded her of what had happened to the intercontinental cable during the war, those reckless decisions made by belligerents in haste. Militaries had destroyed all but one before the haribātna and qēssen stopped them. The final connector, which snaked down from Maqá to Midway and onward to the Southern Continent, had died in the aftermath after centuries spent trying to protect it. It was very hard to find small robots with blades on the seafloor, and an earthquake had finally let them through the perimeter.

Tilōno looked down at Āyiki 7's box. Le needed a better name. *Kalðinbei*, true miracle, sounded as good as any.

"Hey, Kalðī," Tilōno said. The āyiki stirred in the box. "We're going to Maqá."

She looked up, suddenly self-conscious. People were packed into the aisles trying to find seats. She hastily went into the overhead compartment to stuff Tekīya's gift into her carry-on bag. It would be a treat to open in Maqá.

Single passengers typically chose to sit with someone of the same gender. Sselētna would sit with anyone. Tilōno, fresh-pierced and very young, was instantly recognizable as a woman, not a girl. The all-gender car was a chaos of people navigating whom they would and would not sit beside. Her parents would hate that she wasn't in a women's car.

Kalðī sang from inside ler box. Tilōno set her tablet aside, reached down, and pulled the cage into her lap. She uncovered it. They could see each other through the cage. "I can't take you out," she said. "It's too scary in the car."

The āyiki's purple-black-green down was a dun color in the train's low lighting. All three sets of eyes were open wide, searching. "Tekīya shouldn't have left you with me like this, right? Isn't he cruel sometimes?"

Kalðī sang as if assenting. Tilōno looked up. Enough people looked at her, but nobody sat down.

The woman from the kiosk boarded at the front of the car,

facing back towards the mess of people putting away their bags all around Tilōno. Her face was blotchy from crying.

Tilōno sat very still. She looked away from the ō Ćedīsam woman and tried not to glance back. The woman's gaze prickled against her forehead. She stole a glance her way. Their eyes met for a brief second. Tilōno's heart went wild, beating fast in her throat.

The woman stopped beside her. Tilōno stared straight at the back of the chair in front of her. Even Kalðī quieted suddenly, sensory arms poking at the cage.

"You were the Midway girl at the gender initiation ceremony. The librarian." The woman's voice was the smoothest Tilōno had ever heard, as if science had fused oil and soft music and the human vocal tract together.

"Um, yeah." Tilōno turned her head. "You were there."

Tilōno had no memory of this woman from the ritual, just the Registry and the train station. Noblewomen received their initiations alongside commoners because the Gods of gender cared nothing for social ranking, just about the honors due to them. Womanhood and manhood were covenants. Sselē-hood, the neutral position, was bound by no God-oaths.

"Sīyas," the woman said. She clicked her tongue once. "I will sit with you, since I don't have a choice. You're the only one I recognized from the train line. Could you move the tablet?"

Tilōno clicked her tongue reciprocally. She processed the words seconds after Sīyas uttered them. "Oh! Yes." She picked up the tablet and set it down on the cage. "Tilōno."

Sīyas sat down. They smiled at each other. The noblewoman had eyes hued as intensely as fleeting summer flowers or day-sky. *Tilā*, a neologism Tilōno's parents didn't think was good Atarahi. They still insisted *tilā* wasn't a real color. Tilōno's lips parted slightly. Her mind raced through everything she could say.

It all sounded silly and childish.

Sīyas cleared her throat. "You didn't ask how I knew you were a librarian?"

"Um, my Registry profile, right?"

"Your friend. I asked him about you." She chuckled softly. "It's a rare woman who keeps friendships with men after her initiation, especially a haribān."

Tilōno's eyes widened. "You asked him about me?"

"What else was I supposed to do?" Sīyas rolled ler eyes and looked down. "I know it's not socially expected. I don't like doing so much of what is expected of me, either."

Tilōno nodded. Beautiful Sīyas, with her compelling eyes and bewitching voice, at least had the flaw of being socially embarrassing. "Do you mean you talking to a strange haribān like that or sitting next to a Midway woman?"

Sīyas shrugged. "There are other islands besides Midway. What's the animal?"

"A tame hāyiko. An āyiki. Tekīya gave lim to me. I'm supposed to socialize lim," Tilōno said. She had reams of things to say about the āyiki. A person like Sīyas probably didn't want reams.

"I'd like one."

The final boarding announcement came over the intercom. Several hours with this woman sitting beside her. Tilōno forced a smile. Her stomach did flip-flops, and she felt sick. "Maybe someday. Tekīya's hard to talk to when you want things out of him. What do you do, Sīyas?"

"I'm a musician." Sīyas smiled.

"Like, popular music with concerts?"

"My final project, yes. I just graduated from the Owá Conservatory," Sīyas said. She jutted her chin towards the robots racing to place the last of the luggage on the train. "My parents would rather I go into temple composition than secular performance. There's just so much gossip and celebrity worship in the latter."

Tilōno blurted, "I'd pay to see you perform."

"Would you? You haven't even heard my work." Sīyas laughed and leaned back in her seat. The sunlight outside caught on her hair and face. "Nobody has yet. Nobody who's anybody."

Tilōno's entire family consisted of engineers, doctors, and scientists. She thought back to the temple compositions she'd heard, especially the one a pibling had declared *from a new composer* with distaste. That one had been an experimental piece that sounded like wind, offered in the temple of the God who made the weather good during the summer shipping months.

In the data stream, she could have dived into an answer within seconds. Without it, and outside of the library, she felt bare. At least Sīyas liked talking about herself. Tilōno asked questions the entire train ride, comforting Kalðī and chiding herself over a crush on a woman she would never see again.

&❧

The next morning, Tilōno awoke before dawn and left her room in the young professionals' dormitory. The hallway windows were open, leaves caught against the screen rustling as the cold autumn air billowed in. Tilōno shivered. Kalðī followed her, scampering around her legs and cooing in ler sing-song voice.

The morning passed in a haze: Feeding Kalðī raw meet from a bin, standing in line for the shower, taking space in the back of the cramped prayer room to do the sequence for Sa, Sanwū, and Sasnē while she shivered. Thirty professionals lived alongside her, nineteen in the women's section. The lines for everything were long. Everyone stopped to ask about Kalðī.

She ate quickly in the mess hall downstairs. It was Demzang

fare, the things she knew others in Owá ate for breakfast but had rarely experienced herself — hot flatbread pancakes stuffed with savory spices, pickled sea-plants, ribfruit puree, and soup with shaved meat and pulled noodles. There was meat so fresh from the sea that its white pieces still jiggled on the table. The seasoning was unexpectedly sweet and tangy. She didn't eat it.

Weak sunlight flooded through the trees as she walked outside. Maqá smelled like autumn, and she smelled like factory-fresh robes and incense. A train snaked down the road, divided from the wide sidewalk by green space filled with trees, benches, and winter-tolerant ground cover. The train route she needed stopped about a block from the building.

Opening libations at the library had already started by the time she arrived. Wula ō Vousí, the Head Librarian, performed them in front of the public doors accompanied by five singers, a man on a double-reeded sārn, and a sselē beating out the rhythm on a wide-arced ðāde drum. Library staff waited on the steps in silence. Tilōno could not see her new supervisor among them, but she knew what Tilsa looked like from ler network profile.

After the doors opened, she reported to the Head Librarian's office, which looked out over the library's main reading room. Below, robots delivered books to tables, where scholars unpacked their travel bags for a morning of work. Even with the data stream, so many came to use the print collections and be close to the information experts.

Beyond the scholars' space was the public reading room, separated by great arched doors. Public programming for individuals and families happened there, conducted by in-person loreteachers and librarians. It also contained the small shrines to the Triad and the Reed Goddesses frequented by Maqáng students before they ventured into the scholars' reading room or left for their classes in the adjacent buildings. Tilōno had seen that part virtually during her placement interview with human resources. She vaguely remembered a staircase to the upper levels.

"Most of the library is on the other side, through the other window," the head librarian said.

Tilōno turned towards Ussēta Wula and bowed.

Wula had arc-like piercings through each ear, four total, each inscribed with sacred phrases for the Reed Goddesses, and an old, pleasant face, with Mother tattoos on her cheeks for the Goddess Bobes. When she smiled, her eyebrow and forehead piercings glinted in the overhead light. Her curly gray hair and light brown skin meant that her ancestors included the minority Igzarhjenya settlers, not just the Sāqab imperialists, so she had immensely powerful ancestral Gods. The Sāqab had never truly conquered the Igzarhjenya.

Tilōno planted her feet firmly on the ground and cupped her right fist in her left hand at her sternum. She met the Head Librarian's gaze. Her stomach did somersaults, but she breathed through her nervousness. "Thank you for summoning me into service, Ussēta Librarian Wula ō Vousí."

"Ussēta Tilōno," Wula said, "it was expected of you."

The antechamber suddenly felt small. Tilōno made eye contact with Wula's ear. The elder librarian's gaze slithered up and down her body. She had better things to do, Tilōno betted, than spend time with a barely-eighteen initiate. "Thank you all the same."

"I will introduce you to your supervisor, Tilsa ō Naítam." Wula jutted her chin towards the second door. "These are the stairs that lead down into the librarians' section. The Hall of Oracles is not far."

Tilōno had read what she could about Maqá National Library's access policies. The Hall of Oracles had the same human consultation hours as the remainder of the library, with only automata and non-sentient robots staffing after everything closed for the night. The Hall of Oracles required registering to view collections in a separate reading room, and library users could not go into the stacks. Everyone using the collection had their names reported to the government.

She opened the door for Wula and waited for the Head Librarian to go halfway down the stairs before she followed. In the enormous room below, professional librarians and archivists mingled with one another. It was a staging ground for the data stream pods that lay in orderly rows stacked three high. The morning shift was just now diving in. The paging kiosks around the eight doors leading away from the great circular room were lit, and the runners had already started working.

The first door led to science, the symbols of the Thirteen Ways of Knowing emblazoned over its doors. The second led to the medical, genetic, and biotechnology sciences, emblazoned with a modified double helix. The third led to engineering and robotics, attended by the human-like AI library staff and strange-shaped, hummod librarians. The fourth led to the cultural memory center and the heart of the National Library and the inner sanctum of the Triad, where not even an initiate like Tilōno could see the rites performed. That place held the archival and special collections from the beginning of Atara, from the first city plans of Colony Site Five — once Maqaden, now Maqá — to the records from the other six worlds. The original documents were in Marmaḥa and Ịgzarhjemaj, which almost no one could read anymore. The fifth door led to the music and theatrical collections, the sixth to the wealth of fiction and travelogues, and the seventh to the history of the peoples.

The eighth door to their far right led to the Hall of Oracles. Like the other doors, it had one entryway from the librarians' atrium and another from the public rooms.

"Your time will be split between reference and the Hall of Oracles. Each morning, report to the data stream pods. Ussēta Tilsa was generous in only requiring your afternoons," Wula said as they walked. "A fresh graduate who can stay in for five hours is an asset, and we want to keep you at skill should the future bring you to one of the reference librarian positions. Try your ID, please."

Tilōno rushed forward to open the door to the Hall of Oracles. She swiped her standard ID, and it clicked to unlock satisfyingly. As the Head Librarian entered the hallway, Tilōno bowed her head.

Gnawing sounds came from the walls on either side, so unlike compact shelving noises that Tilōno hesitated at the threshold. Wula looked back at her and said, "We're repairing the ventilation systems. The space to our left is mechanical. Pay it no mind."

Tilōno followed. They swiped through a door at the end of the long corridor. Wula stepped through without even a glance up.

Human resources hadn't shown Tilōno the Hall of Oracles during her remote tour. It was like no library collection Tilōno had seen before. Eighteen tables lay on either side of the central aisle, their surfaces carved with celestial sky maps. At the room's perimeter behind and in front of her, collections of bound journals and treatises lay behind locked wire doors, which did nothing but make the collection look intimidating. On the right were three separate doors, but Tilōno couldn't see anything but the warm light spreading out over the floor.

To the left beyond the reading room, she spied compact shelving that went far above her head through a semitransparent glass wall. The only sound from within was the whir of the shelves as they moved and the chitter of the robotic book scanners.

The vaulted ceiling was intricate. Tilōno envisioned the amount of time it must have taken the artists to paint each detailed divine figure, cross-referencing against temples all across the world to get their iconographies correct. Each of Atara's divination sites was mapped out in polar hemispheres of Atara's North and South, and the Gods looked down over each half. Midway was barely visible on the map, but it had only three oracular sites. Demza had twenty-eight major oracular sites and hundreds of minor ones. Her gaze was drawn to the island archipelagos dotting the wide ocean. A strange symbol had been placed on one. It must have been Black Sands, the most prized and secretive of all of the ritual sites.

The Head Librarian yelled, "Tilsa! Ussēta! I have the initiate for you!"

Something clattered to the floor in the closest office. A sselē at least a decade and a half older than Tilōno peeked out, hands frantically rolling ler sleeves down. Ler scholarly robes were not folded properly around ler neck. Le wasn't as decorated as Wula, but ler face bore markings from nearly all of the same mystery milestones as the older librarian. Le wore ler hair in a popular sselē style, in a crown-like circular braid around ler head, ghost-light beads glowing against ler dark brown hair.

The robes looked lived-in, unlike Tilōno's or the Head Librarian's. This was a practicing librarian, regardless of administrative title. Tilōno made a palm-against-two-fingers salute, arms in front of her chest. Tilsa repeated it.

"Is this the girl? Woman, sorry." Tilsa asked.

"Yes," Tilōno said. She bowed her head towards her hands, then lowered her arms to her sides.

The Head Librarian nodded. "The young are the future of our profession, an adamantine chain that we must work to protect from the winds that weather memory away." The words were stiff, likely quoted from some text that Tilōno did not know.

Tilsa gave the Head Librarian a smile that turned hollow before it reached ler eyes.

Tilōno looked down again before le looked at her.

Tilsa said, "You can leave me with her, then. Thank you for your visit."

The Head Librarian smiled. "Good day." She left without a second glance.

Tilōno remained at attention in front of Tilsa, who paced as soon as the Head Librarian shut the door. It was as if le were sizing up whether she could tie her robes properly. Tilsa clicked ler tongue and nodded slowly as if satisfied. Le stopped directly in front of her, hands clasped at the knuckles.

Tilōno made eye contact. Tilsa had eyes like the woman on the train, deep and sky-hued, rich with that pigment that was not a color, as if the sky had melted into lim.

"You are the apprentice librarian who can last for over five hours in the data stream," Tilsa said. It wasn't a question. Ler brow furrowed. "Do you know how the Hall of Oracles conducts its affairs? What did the Head Librarian tell you?"

"I am here to learn," Tilōno said.

Tilsa snickered. "Right. Whatever she told you, I asked to have you for full days, and that request was denied. Afternoons are busier, so thank the Gods I have you then." Le snapped ler fingers and gestured for Tilōno to follow.

They went to the doorway to the compact shelving. Tilsa pointed with ler chin and said, "Why do we have bots scanning the shelves if the collection is closed? Those are data stream query robots doing the same scans they do elsewhere. Why are they here?"

Tilōno winced. "I don't know."

"National security." Tilsa turned ler head towards Tilōno. "We have the largest collection of materials that has an S designation. People who can look things up remotely have security clearance — black, indigo, violet, and green. Politicians and international operatives. The two collectives, although they usually send someone in person. Kaleḥ, the Qēssa-leader, visits. He does not send a delegation."

Tilōno looked up the vast, almost cavernous expanse of shelves. Row after row of book stared down at her. "Most people have to come in person or send questions? It's mediated?"

Tilsa murmured a prayer to Sa under ler breath before responding. "Obviously. It means we have no runners. You're the closest thing to one. Questions at the violet clearance level and below are logged in the register. They are not private. We have to do everything, so your clearance is green now. Congratulations on being politically boring." Le looked up and down the stacks. "The collection has an international scope. We're a designated national repository. Understaffed, so you wouldn't know from the look of the place. They gave me you instead of hiring a librarian to fill an open position."

Tilōno glanced at the opaque black shelving, which marked the classification ranges with digital and analog inserts at nearly eye level. *Politically boring.* What did that mean for the people who worked in the collection?

"I'm waiting."

People would want oracles from abroad, if only to know what the Gods told others. "Because the cable failed?"

"We collected print copies before. It was an intergovernmental decree with standards developed by the qēssen and haribātna. The minimum print holdings were divided among libraries on each continent to maximize accessibility." Tilsa snickered. "The data cable failed after I was appointed to my first position here, perhaps by two months. I was twenty-five and not very prepared for that."

Tilōno tried to envision Tilsa at twenty-five and couldn't. She shifted from foot to foot and turned to look at the reading area. It was silent, empty, void. Tilōno would have preferred gate counts and an assignment, perhaps a show of the materials the collection contained. It couldn't all be in compact shelving if this were partially a proceedings repository. Tilsa had not mentioned any offsite storage.

With a jerk of ler head, Tilsa showed Tilōno out to the main floor. Their footsteps echoed. It felt as if the silent Gods over their heads watched, hidden in the humanoid forms people had given them. Tilōno's stomach writhed.

"I will be frank with you," Tilsa said. "I have held this management position for only two years, and *that* because I know the collection nearly as well as the Director who came before me."

"What happened to lim?"

"Le died suddenly." Tilsa pursed ler lips together. Le surveyed the offices and beckoned Tilōno towards the central door. "Be careful, Tilōno."

The cataloging department had a backlog, not unusual for a library. A woman working at one of the standing tables swayed as she danced to implant headphones, a luxury purchase Tilōno couldn't afford for years. A hummod worked at a nearby table, its surface dusty and covered in the slough of old bindings and pages that had withered to brittle nothingness. Two helper AI bots snaked along the floor. They had humanlike faces. When one smiled at her, she looked away.

"Ussēta Hūtong is our Lead Cataloger, and he liaises to the preservation unit."

The hummod raised his head and focused on Tilōno. He had tech-covered eyes that meant his organic ones had been destroyed, piercings coming out of his flesh at odd angles just beneath the transition to real skin. It was hard to tell where to make eye contact. Still, the smile happened. Hūtong's arms, covered with initiatory symbols, marked him as a member of a religious sect that had been outlawed in Owá for disturbing the peace with lewd processions. Obviously, Maqá was different enough that someone like that could get clearance. Tilōno bowed her head.

"The woman is Ussēta Hāyin, the Associate Cataloger," Hūtong intoned.

Hāyin smiled broadly. When she leaned against the table, her chest pressed against it, dimpling her scholar uniform's pattern, a stylized calligraphic print from a text about library ethics. "This is the young one who has come to us?"

"Who will be apprenticing with me." Tilsa nodded, ler expression grave.

"That's good," Hūtong said. "Will she ultimately perform your former reference duties?"

Tilsa shrugged. "That will take time."

"We're heading out of summer-season," Hūtong said.

Tilsa looked at Tilōno. "We're at our busiest in summer. The general population doesn't understand how long it takes for us to process new materials — we're inundated with questions as soon as the new shipments arrive from the boats. Don't worry about that now — just file it for later in your mind, yes?"

This new mentor had a personality wholly unlike Tekīya, who would have taken her through at least three self-deprecating stories. A pang hit her in the chest, and her smile faltered. She covered by bowing slightly to Hāyin, whose smile reached her eyes as soon as the gesture was complete.

A gong-like bell rang.

"The library is open," Tilsa said. "We will check in around

lunchtime? I need to bring the new hire to the Head of Reference."

"Yes," Hūtong said.

Tilsa snapped ler fingers twice and nodded at Tilōno. The repeated gesture would have been rude in Owá, but Owáng people complained incessantly that Maqá's residents had no manners. Tilōno followed.

It was too early for her to form an opinion of any of these new people just yet.

CHAPTER THREE

Data scattered like stardust.

Questions came through the system like the final breaths of the dead and dying. It was easy to let them unravel her, to lose herself in the factoids about Atara's great war or geologic information about the sand, taiga, and tundra.

Being in the data stream was like using herself as a prism. She bent in all directions, spliced apart until all that remained was her knifelike core cutting through and dissolving into the infinite multitude of documents, definitions, and referrals.

The general reference pods' questions could be anything from nonspecialists. It meant pushing and pulling her way through the entire library, fighting for queue priority with bots in literature, science, medicine, and beyond. Network-connected people on all parts of the continent, national and international, queried the library via network interfaces, most if it in text format. Maqá National Library only gave the true VR sim to seasoned librarians.

Tilōno's session ended abruptly, just as she was a half-dissolved echo of herself, drowning in the rush of information through her synapses. The pod ran through its cooldown routine. Everything always seemed so slow when coming back into the awareness of being flesh, orienting herself to the sweaty fingers, toes, and limbs of her real body. A robotic attendant helped her leave.

It was halfway through her fourth hour in the pod. Plunging into data left her body hungry and a bit shaky. It was too late to catch lunch with the other staff in the Hall of Oracles. She needed to go outside.

Tilōno had the right to a longer break to recover from the stream. She registered the extended lunch and left the library for the sun-drenched noonday promenade. It was clear, the sky only swelling with clouds close to the far horizon, so the light came warm once she left the building's chilly shadow.

The cross-street eateries lay halfway down Scholars' Walk, past the Maqá National Library, Conservatory, and School of Science and Technology. Most restaurants close to the intellectual campus were packed with students just let out of classes and scholars taking breaks from their time in laboratories, lecture halls, discussion rooms, and at library desks or in information kiosks. The air smelled like grilled meat, soup, and yeasted bread.

Tilōno waited at the crossroads, undecided about where to go. They all sold the same Demzang food, from lighter to heavier fare. She craved the seafood and flatbreads of Midway, a blast of childhood nostalgia hitting her full force on the street where people walked and discussed philosophy or music or a thousand million other academic topics. Nobody was alone. She was lonely.

She knew no one in Maqá.

With a sigh, she walked along the row until she found the least crowded restaurant. The lunch offering was grilled seafood with pounded ribfruit congee and pickles. It was good enough to fill her up on work days until she could go home to see Tekīya and her family.

Tilōno tethered her tablet into the wall and responded to her family's Registry messages with upbeat, short comments. They didn't need to know that she was eating alone or that she was homesick. Maqá had nice sunsets over the water. She'd tell her family that.

When will you attend a matchmaker dance? Instead of answering her mother's question, Tilōno went into her workplace queue and checked her schedule. Afternoons in the Hall of Oracles were starting to grow on her.

She finished her lunch quickly and arrived back fifteen minutes before her Registry-anticipated return time, a queue of questions waiting for her and a roomful of querents to supervise and help.

People consulted oracles for the uncertain pieces of their lives, and Tilōno sympathized with them. She tried not to show her eagerness to switch from in-person help to addressing the data stream queue.

Tilōno entered the compact shelving halfway through the afternoon. As she answered questions, she picked up adjacent volumes just to read them. The books' oracular queries were fascinating: Who stole a set of prized pillowcases. Advice on which young man to accept as a husband, with additional information about the choices' spermatozoa viability. A sselē asking whether or not to pursue a court case. Someone labeled *the querent* with a poetic creative block. Two hikers puzzling over whether they should believe the geologic reports about avalanche prognosis in an area they wanted to visit. A young man speculating over whether someone had stolen an antique wind-up toy inherited from his grandfather. Another sselē wondering about the likelihood of a romantic relationship working out between lim and a woman with two young children, one with a disability. A man in grief over a marriage that wouldn't continue into a romantic relationship. Two young women seeking advice about a pibling's mental illness after a failed intervention. A woman in despair after failing public service examinations three times in a row. Someone whose cancer kept recurring.

One of the questions had been referred to her from the priority queue, green-level clearance, requesting pages 107-110 from *Records from the Oracle at Tuða*'s Spring 4299. Individuals with that permission level could use the bots, and they often did to preserve discretion, but this one was flagged PAGINATION ERROR.

The querent had provided no request details. She opened the volume and checked the pages.

Someone had razored them out.

Tilōno set the volume down and picked up the one beside it, Autumn 4298. She summoned a bot down and tethered in so she could access the data stream on her tablet. Photographs of Tuðá helped Tilōno put things into perspective. The oracular site there was the size of an entire city district, its perimeter drawn tight against the pollution of mundane life. Hundreds consulted the oracle each of its opening days, and thousands came to the rituals of purification for the oracular vessel.

Autumn 4298 had no missing pages. She checked the headings. After records of oracular consultations from the public came the ones given to an oracle's sponsoring families. Most were in the nobility. These were undirected oracles that read like a stream of consciousness narrative, a direct window into a divinity monologuing about anything it thought a querent might care about.

She checked Autumn 4299 next. The noble families lay in the same order, but the pages allocated to each varied. Cross-referenced against them, the pages in Spring 4298 must have covered two-thirds of the ō Ćedīsam oracles and the beginning of the oracles for ō Đōtam.

She stacked the volumes up, untethered her tablet, and left the stacks. The robot clicked and clattered back up the shelves. As soon as she left her row, the bookshelves started moving.

Tilōno brought the books to Tilsa's office, where the sselē stood going over reports on the large tablet desk in front of lim.

"Ussēta Tilōno," le said.

"Ussēta Director Tilsa," Tilōno responded automatically. "May I ask something?"

Tilsa's weight shifted. Le smoothed wrinkles in ler scholar's uniform and met Tilōno's eyes, catching her in a gaze that seemed to last an eternity before le looked away. "Yes."

Tilōno approached the table with the books. Tilsa locked ler screen. "Someone cut pages out of one of the volumes from the Tuðáng oracular reports. I pulled two close by to see which pages were missing."

"Okay. Set them down."

Tilōno opened the volume. "I had a question referred from the AI robot. Green-level." She thumbed her fingers to the missing pages and slid the book over to lim.

"Shut the door." Tilsa touched the pages' stumps delicately. Le frowned. "And it's the only one? Are the others fine?"

"I only checked two." Tilōno slid the door shut.

Her supervisor's eyes narrowed. Le tapped ler fingers against the book pages. "We'd have to know the donor list and monetary values for each of the families in that half-year period. The order goes by which family donated the most money."

"Ō Ćedīsam is in the same place in the other volumes."

"The autumn volumes of 4298 and 4299. You have the spring volume of 4299." Tilsa squeezed ler eyes shut and breathed. "You'd have to check volumes from every spring, Ussēta."

Tilōno's face grew hot.

"Some families have different financial commitments in each season. The temple would have the records, not us," Tilsa continued.

I didn't need to learn the economics of how oracular sites are managed during my advanced degree, Tilōno thought. Tilsa wasn't Tekīya. She'd have voiced her opinion if le were more like him. "Do you want me to pull *all* of the volumes, then? For—"

"Right, you might as well check every volume going back ten years, just for consistency's sake. Stop at the autumn volume of 4300. We just got that earlier in the season," Tilsa said. "How long have you spent on this reference question?"

"About half an hour."

"Okay, so not too long. You'll need to send the querent a note about the delay. Le's plugged into the network?"

"Yes, I think." Tilōno frowned.

Tilsa sighed. "Don't tell lim that it's missing. Say that the information is not available in that volume yet."

"Why?"

"It doesn't look good to have people razoring out important oracular information for the nobility, especially after the government stopped allowing private copies," Tilsa said. Le leaned in and glanced towards the door. "It's done this way in Demza because we had a problem with oracles during the war. The old heads of the department warned me. It's politically delicate."

Tilōno nodded. "And I can't write about this digitally anywhere, then."

"No."

Her brow furrowed. Tilsa closed the defaced volume and removed it to an empty library cart.

"Are you okay?" Tilōno asked.

"I'm fine." Tilsa shook ler head and snorted. "The pages weren't destroyed, just taken. The vandal was careless. Almost all oracular sites print on nābimī, so good fucking luck getting rid of the evidence without an industrial grinder."

Nābimī was one of the final interplanetary materials innovations before the ships all grounded, inspired by inter-civilization clay tablets on Ameisa — a material that fire preserved rather than taking away. As far as Tilōno knew, only Atara took nābimī seriously, and it had never gone into wide production on the other planets. Most information about the other worlds she had learned over the years had come from Tekīya or history class, and given the grounding of space transit, she'd never need details. She knew from him that the ascendant culture on Maðz had a heavy cultural attachment to traditional paper-making.

On Atara, nābimī was used for most books — which limited the print run sizes, but made copies durable and nearly indestructible. Now that all information had to pass on ship, it also protected materials from water damage.

"But whoever it was brought in a diamond razor," Tilōno said. "If it *was* a library user, does le know that le can't put it in with normal waste? A bot would have caught it and flagged nābimī in the municipal system."

"You don't desecrate a temple of learning and knowledge without first doing significant research on how." Tilsa shook ler head.

Tilsa did not say, *It was library staff,* but Tilōno considered the possibility. It wasn't impossible for someone outside of bookwork to have a nābimī-capable razor, but a single razor cost more than a month of her wage. Even with immense resources, it had taken Tekīya three months to procure one for her in the menagerie's archives. "I'll pull the volumes, then."

"Do it quickly and go through them in my office," Tilsa responded. It was almost a confirmation of Tilōno's suspicions, but not quite.

Tilsa could have stolen them, she thought.

"Are you sure?"

"Yes. The catalogers won't want to bother with this." Tilsa scratched ler arm through ler sleeve and glanced down at the passive, pool-like black screen on the table. It was a mirror while off, albeit distorted. "I have a meeting with my supervisor in about fifteen minutes, and I will leave you in here with one of the bots."

Tilōno nodded. "Thank you."

She walked back out into the reading room. Hāyin and Hūtong's voices carried softly into the space from their cataloging room. Work banter.

The spider-like bot almost swam down the compact shelving as it gripped them with its thin arms, as graceful as a fish swimming in the sea or a bird in the air. It occupied a space near Tilōno's problem *Records from the Oracle at Tuðá*, its eyes rapidly scanning something from one of the minor cavern oracles in a small town in Tuðáqazi, just a hundred kilometers from Tuðá proper. She entered the row and walked confidently up to it.

"Did you see something?" she whispered.

It lifted its gaze from the book to Tilōno. The mirrored eyes seemed vast, almost endless, and the robot's limbs hovered in the air. It crawled closer to her and came up until its sensory units were just millimeters from hers.

The scanning AI was not smart, and it couldn't speak. Her

stomach curled into knots when she looked at it, though, and tried to imagine what it saw in her when its entire program was trained on locating books to scan materials for the data grid or to answer basic questions not passed on to humans.

It tapped one of its hind limbs against six volumes from *Records from the Oracle at Tuðá*, not all in order, and definitely not random. Four of them came from the spring records, two from the autumnal ones. The earliest was Spring 4291.

"Are pages missing from those?" she asked. Her breath clouded its cool lenses.

Its leg hit the same volumes all over again. "Thank you."

The robot turned abruptly from her and went back to its business in the system, plugging in at the data connection overhead for a brief moment to receive its summons for the next information requests. She drew the six volumes one by one. They all had missing pages. A seventh, done for control, came from Autumn 4291. It was pristine.

She brought the heavy volumes back out into the main floor. Two people milled near the entrance in need of assistance. With Tilsa leaving, that would fall to her. Retrieving other volumes would have to wait.

὎

She didn't stop serving library users until late afternoon. Eighteen people sat at the desks under the robots' watchful eyes. Once it looked like nobody needed human help, she retrieved the other volumes and left the main room for Tilsa's office.

Tilōno left the door cracked just in case someone had a question. She opened each of the volumes and puzzled her way through what was in the missing sections. She checked family names first — missing family oracles could have been ō Atesī, ō

Ćedīsam, or ō Ðōtam, based on what was consistently in that section.

Ō Atesī and ō Ćedīsam had an ongoing rivalry at times, as the sselētna in each family vied for the same public offices. They wouldn't send rivals to steal oracles — that would have been too labor-intensive. She had barely heard of ō Ðōtam before that day.

The oracular indices, modeled after subject headings in library collections, were twenty thick pages at the back of each book, the text so small that she needed a magnifying glass to read it. The subjects covered ranged across politics, government, and family. Tilōno made note of the ones related to the missing pages on a piece of scrap paper.

- *Oracles — Travel — Sightseeing — Private Vehicle Tours.*
- *Oracles — Travel — Vehicles — Boat.*
- *Oracles — Politics — Warnings.*
- *Oracles — Politics — Marriage.*
- *Oracles — Government (Demzang) — Negotiations.*
- *Oracles — Government (Demzang) — Chancellorship.*
- *Oracles — Families — Warnings.*
- *Oracles — Families — Purification.*
- *Oracles — Families — Noble Houses.*
- *Oracles — Families — Financial.*
- *Oracles — Families — Marriage.*
- *Oracles — Estates.*

It would have been engrossing to read the oracles had she not been searching for clues about the missing pages. The stream-of-consciousness advice in the text felt like eavesdropping on an elder speaking intimately, and without membership in the family ler words were directed towards, the monologue was too cryptic to understand.

She gradually became aware of the lights dimming towards closing time and the softness of footsteps at the door. She glanced up at Tilsa as le entered, surprised at the weariness in that face.

"Have you found anything?"

"If everyone followed this advice to the letter, we would have mass chaos," Tilōno said softly. She nodded at a stack of volumes to her right. "Those are the ones missing pages. I've made notes."

Tilsa shut the door to the main floor. "Not everyone will. That's why oracles are effective — everyone has access to them, but only the Gods know who will heed what they say — and among Gods, the Lord of Time and the Weaver of Fate most of all." Le tethered in ler tablet.

Tilōno stood upright and stretched her arms over her head. Her neck and breastbone cracked. As she lowered her arms, she reached for the paper with her right hand and passed it over to Tilsa.

This time, her boss didn't frown. Ler brow furrowed. "Ō Ðōtam is one of the Five Families. They were all exiled to the Māro Islands about a century ago, but still heed oracles on the mainland. Cable still reaches Māro. It's not so far from the mainland that it ever broke. None of the automata cut it, either."

"What were the exile charges?"

"Political opponents of the post-war regime. Each of the families liked the debauchery they remembered from the High Empire days — the feasts, the technology, the wanton wealth inequality. It was a political lesson here." Tilsa smirked. "It is probably why we have the nobility in Demza and not on Midway — they understood clearly what they would not be allowed to do. Everyone wants stability and meaningful lives. That, and the haribānōqi or qēssang presences here in Maqá deter wrongheaded thinking."

Haribātna, Tilōno thought. The Owá stronghold where Tekīya lived was among many of their secondary estates around the world. The main estate was in Maqá. "Do the haribātna or qēssen receive copies of the oracular reports?"

"I don't know," Tilsa said. "If they did, we wouldn't have access to them. Some of them come here to consult oracle registers. They're the only ones who know what the oracle says at Black Sands."

Her heart pounded almost in her throat. "I might know someone who can help."

"We are not personally involving ourselves in political intrigue among the nobility," Tilsa said gently. Le set the paper back on the table. "Even if it *was* a reference question, you need to verify that the information is not here."

"Why not?"

"This is not like other units, Ussēta Tilōno." Tilsa pointed at the door with ler chin. "We take down names and identification because the government has demanded to know the identities of everyone who consults oracles in Demza's libraries. If this was done by a member of the national administration, le — or they — will know if we *do* answer this."

"So we keep the identity of the person who asked it via data stream?"

"It will probably be in my weekly report." Le shook ler head. "Leave it, Tilōno."

"What about cameras?"

Tilsa indicated the door with ler head again and lowered ler voice. "You do know who is out at those tables? Do you think they want video so anyone can pattern-match the lip movements? Everything recorded can potentially be used."

She pursed her lips together and envisioned herself sneaking in to check the weekly report using Tilsa's borrowed identification. Le'd know. The authorities would question *lim* if anything untoward happened. There had to be another way, through Tekīya. "The lack of cameras still seems reckless. Robots obviously can't do everything."

Tilsa's voice became the barest of whispers, "You need to know who they are."

"Doesn't it bother you that someone came into our temple and defiled it?"

"Of course it does." Tilsa pressed ler thumbs against ler temples. In Classical Atarahi, le said, "Đwō uk kutōqi helēna bēkihabodćoto." *Today, you dove into dangerous waters.*

Tilōno shook her head and said, "I do not dive so deep," in Demaí. "Is someone blackmailing the Hall of Oracles? Is that why you won't do anything?"

Tilsa shook ler head. Le leaned ler hands against the table and frowned down at the books lain out in front of them. Slowly, le picked one of them up and opened it, fingers moving steadily along the pages. "How discreet can you be about making inquiries?"

"Very d—"

"You're an eighteen-year-old woman," Tilsa said. "Who do you know?"

"A haribān in Owá, a friend." Tilōno lowered her gaze. "His name is Tekīya."

"His?"

"Yes."

"It's not easy to find one of them who has done Sāqab gender rituals," Tilsa said sharply, almost accusingly.

She'd asked that question at twelve. It was taboo to say anything else to Tilsa, namely that Tekīya had become a haribān just before undergoing gender initiation — that he'd passed every test of manhood and had undergone the initiation ritual itself while in the early stages of the muakanua, which was technically profaning a mystery. Haribātna and qēssen could not undergo gender initiation after the sickness that made them what they were unless an oracle explicitly told an individual that le could, and most of them never sought that out because their flesh rejected new tattoos and piercings after the muakanua sickness had abated. A sselē would never have accorded someone like Tekīya the honor of *he*.

They stared tensely at each other until Tilōno turned away. It was the role she needed to fulfill in the conversation. "I need to talk to him anyway about how Kalðī is doing. Kalðī is an animal he gave me for friendship." There was no word in Demaí or Classical Atarahi for *pet* apart from the one Tekīya had made up. "He owes me."

Tilsa winced. "When I was your age, I knew a qēssa. Vaymi, if you ever meet lim — an Igzarhjenya, a man in their society, but le never used our words for initiates. We saw concerts together. There's a reason we grew apart after I was no longer so young. People in those hive minds sometimes have their own personalities, sometimes not. They don't age or die under ordinary circumstances. It makes them strange. That's nothing about our specific problem. It's just life advice."

"Tekīya is a haribān. They're calmer."

"Think like a mortal, Ussēta Tilōno." Le sighed. "Fine. Flag the question — say you couldn't find it. That will cover for us. We can follow up on our own. If the haribān can be discreet, go to him and ask for help. If not, we are back where we started — missing textual pieces, no clear and legal way to escalate. Indigo clearance could. I'm not convinced about using illegal means yet."

"What would those be?"

"Unlicensed necrobibliomancy."

Tilōno gritted her teeth and nodded. "Right. No necrobibliomancy." She filed the word away. It had appeared in library ritual texts as something possible for advanced initiates. There was no telling what a librarian at Tilsa's level could do, what le was barred from doing, and what the Gods demanded of lim.

"Where do we put the texts for now?"

"I have a locked bookcase under the tablescreen," le said.

Tilōno gathered the books together and handed them one by one to Tilsa. She knew better than to ask if their changed location would be reflected in the holdings data. Anyone who needed these wouldn't find them — the bots would turn up empty.

δ♦

The following afternoon, Tilōno walked down Scholars' Walk in search of food. Her stomach growled, and her head felt light. A high-priority request from someone in the government had come in near the end of her pod shift while Tilsa was in meetings, so the Head of Reference had pulled her out to go assist with it in the Hall of Oracles.

The cry, "Tilōno! Midway lady!" caught her completely off-guard.

Tilōno stopped walking towards food and looked from left to right. Her heart beat fast. It was a female voice. It wasn't someone from her lodgings, she was certain of it.

Her gaze fell on Sīyas, standing only a few meters away, every part of her animated by a boisterous joy. She carried a flute case in her right hand and a thick packet of music scores in her left. She rode a wide-bed motorized skateboard, which responded elegantly to her feet as she slowed it down. She was one of the few on Scholars' Walk dressed like a civilian.

"I thought that was you!"

Tilōno fought to make herself smile. At a tilt of the skateboard,

Sīyas was suddenly very close, nearly touching her. Tilōno's autumn coat grew clammy against her skin.

"Yes," Tilōno said.

Sīyas nodded. "How's the library?"

"Getting adjusted," Tilōno murmured. She cleared her throat. "I'm, um, learning. Your music?"

"I had a meeting with some students about a performance," Sīyas said matter-of-factly. She tossed her hair away from her face and smiled widely. "It went over. What are you doing? Is the library still open, or does it close early here?"

"I'm getting a late lunch," Tilōno said. She kept her gaze on Sīyas' face, away from the woman's body. Neither of them had swelled much into breasts yet, anyway, without having kids. Sīyas wasn't nearly as distracting as Hāyin.

Sīyas nodded. "Here?"

"Yes—"

"But it's so crowded!"

Tilōno smirked. "I'm eating alone, so it doesn't matter if—"

The composer nodded. "It's not like conversation could be held here, anyway, I agree. There's a small place about five blocks away from the scholars' district, not far. How long do you have?"

"An hour?"

"Come with me, then."

Tilōno looked at the skateboard. It had enough room for both of them if they stood close enough to each other. Even the thought of it made a knot deep in Tilōno's belly.

"What?" Sīyas asked.

Tilōno shook her head. "Nothing. What do you want to talk about? What didn't we say on the train?"

They met each other's eyes. Sīyas' smile faltered. She shuffled the papers into her right hand and held tightly onto the instrument. With her other hand, she pulled at Tilōno's sleeve. "It would be nice to talk to you, that's all. A friendly face. The young woman from the train."

To most people she assisted, Tilōno was that librarian at the other end of the data connection, the disembodied being who could help them with their work, leisure, or family needs. A trickle of questions that morning had come from the same people over and over, as if bound together by loneliness, yearning for just any human to connect with.

The strange thing about that was that few people spent much time alone. There were people everywhere, especially in cities, and *especially* in multigenerational family houses. Tilōno hoped that Sīyas truly meant that she wanted companionship. This could be a political entanglement.

"Okay," Tilōno said. She shuffled herself up close to Sīyas and climbed on behind her.

Sīyas put one arm around Tilōno's midsection and pulled her close. The woman's body was soft, like clouds, and Tilōno was so small beside her.

"You can't lock your knees," Sīyas said.

"Oh. Sorry."

Tilōno bent them. She still nearly fell as Sīyas revved the board. They passed wave after wave of human crowds on either side, oscillating as if they rode a skiff and the wide sidewalk was the sea. Sīyas dug her fingernails into the back of Tilōno's robe as they came to a stop at the next intersection, the board humming impatiently while they waited for a surface train to pass by.

The stately and pretentious educational and cultural heritage buildings gave way to a normal Maqáng neighborhood, first-floor shops below professional dormitory housing, family homes, and multistory recreation centers. Gone, too, were the tailors and fabric-sellers for all sorts of scholars' robes, each purchase verified against Registry profiles for academic entitlements.

Panel skateboards fit in here, even if Sīyas' skateboard had cushioned shock absorbers and hand-painted scenes from novels on it. A few other people rode smaller ones, generally brushed metal and textured standing pads.

They stopped in front of a restaurant called Quickening. About half of its fifteen tables lay empty, and the remaining people clustered around their bowls of red oil, pulled noodles, and condiments, broth simmering in wide pots at each table's center. It wasn't Demzang food, but Urang. Unlike Demza, Ural consisted of many plateaus and gorges, taiga and tundra, glaciers and cold rivers and deserts. Demza had more rain and snow. Its cold-tolerant rainforests covered over half of the country.

Sīyas smiled at Tilōno. "Could you hold the board?"

Tilōno stepped off of the board and picked it up. It was lighter than she expected. "You like Urang food?"

"You don't?"

"I've never had it."

Maqá was only a hundred kilometers from the border. Owá was deep in Demzang.

They went in and took a table. Tilōno rested the skateboard against a wall and went into the back to wash her hands. The bathrooms were nice, the restaurant roomy enough to segregate by gender.

When she went back out, Sīyas had already ordered. The noodles gleamed in the overhead light, and the woman's long, thick fingers tapped against the table's surface as if they would gallop away if Sīyas didn't focus on them. Tilōno sat down across from her.

"Wow."

Sīyas said, "My mother has a nobility marriage with an Urang official. I am half Urang."

Tilōno nodded. The nobility didn't practice visiting marriages, but made spousal agreements about whose house the other would join. Most married among themselves, and everyone among them descended from both the Sāqab nobility who had come over from the now-fallen Empire and those given nobility for bravery in the colony's early days.

It seemed stifling to have a marriage that never expired, to need to see another person every day instead of just in the conjugal rooms when both in the partnership needed to fulfill the contractual obligation to have children. People had their private lives, their family duties, their work choices, and their lovers.

She became aware of the wince plastered on her face. "Sorry, um." She paused. "I was just thinking. Not about Ural or anything. You're the first member of the nobility I've ever met beyond just in passing."

"Right, and you're a Midway chick."

"What's that supposed to mean?" Tilōno followed Sīyas' lead and dipped a forkful of noodles in condiments. The meat and sauce oozed off of the translucent, chewy fibers. She chewed slowly to keep from frowning.

Sīyas slurped noodles and meat into her mouth and daintily wiped a fleck of pulled oil from her chin with one swipe of the thumb. "You don't have a nobility anymore."

"I'm from Owá," Tilōno said. She spun noodles around the fork's three tines, careful not to spill any of them over the handle. Pulling up the thin shreds of meat worked better this time.

"I told my family I sat next to a Midway woman on the train. Do you know what they said?" Sīyas set her fork down and put her elbows on the table. She leaned in towards Tilōno and rested her head on her hands. "'It's good to put the past behind us.' Weird, right?"

Tilōno swallowed a forkful of noodles. Her hand twitched for the small reader in her scholars' robes, which had a clock that could tell the time. "People from Midway don't think much about what happened, just everyone else. Can we talk about something else?"

"Aren't you worried that someday, everyone on Castaway Island will come back for you?"

"They're rich people without any money, so they're only as dangerous as everyone else now." Tilōno shrugged her shoulders. "The Council now performs their ritual roles. It's—"

"Your founders ate elders' hearts." Sīyas scrunched her face up.

Sīyas was trying to get a rise out of her, but to what end, Tilōno couldn't say. She studied the other young woman's curves, her plump fingers, and the small birthmark on her neck. Sīyas was beautiful and not used to people saying no. Tilōno could tell that much.

"Tell me about what your parents are doing for matchmaking," Tilōno said. "It matters a lot to you, right? Having to pick someone with a lifetime in mind."

The right side of Sīyas' face curled up into a snicker, and she dipped her noodles in sauce. "They told me not to visit the singles' clubs in town. I go to Ural in five months to stay with some cousins, prepare for an Urang musical debut, and find a spouse."

"My aunt Xōqiyi says that the advantage of common marriages is that you can see a man a few times, get pregnant, and then find appropriate companions. People in noble marriages fight." Her aunt had never said that *exactly*. Everyone Tilōno knew was convinced that ordinary marriages were good because they didn't demand too much of a young person just establishing limself in the world. In the data stream, Tilōno sometimes answered questions about other worlds' histories, where childbearing and love were intertwined. The visiting marriage system on Atara was practiced by anyone with sense because it was the best way to organize society.

"Fighting happens in all families."

Tilōno twisted her noodles around the fork and murmured, "Yes, of course, it always happens. Just not in ways that matter nationally. If you draw everyone in power from the same small group—"

"Midway's system was fucked up," Sīyas said. "We'd never do that here."

Tilōno nodded. Demza's last five chancellors were all sselētna from the nobility, with only one sselē from among the common class within the past century. There had been three women and four men out of the number, too. Fifty five-year terms, forty-three people. "Are you looking for someone to visit the singles' dances with you?"

Sīyas grimaced. "Maybe." She leaned forward, large breasts dimpling against the table. "Actually, I'm interested in your work."

Tilōno's chest tightened. *Here we go*, she thought.

"One of my piblings, Bēhel, was saying yesterday that ler reference request failed. I was trying to find you for ler benefit. Le doesn't want to go in person. It's a delicate matter, whatever it is."

Tilōno fought to keep her face neutral. "I'm not sure I can help you with that."

Sīyas shook her head. She slurped noodles up fast, splattering red oil everywhere. Tilōno flinched backward to avoid droplets headed for her robes. "No," Sīyas said, "it's about oracles. It's where you *work*. I went to your profile."

"I do work there." She imagined Sīyas at breakfast with her family talking about nothing in particular — then the reference question and the memory of Tilōno on the train.

"I waited for you outside for *hours*, Tilōno." Sīyas kissed the air. "You evaded me for so long!"

"What do you want me to do?"

"It has to be there. The answer. We just need four pages out of some oracular reports." Sīyas set down her fork. "My elders don't know that I've asked. Bēhel looked angry. You're cute, and I don't want this all to land on *you*."

Would Tilsa have been ready to tell Sīyas the truth? Tilōno let it burn inside of herself. Arguably, Sīyas didn't look distressed. She could still eat. There were no tears in her eyes. She'd called Tilōno *cute*. "I'll see what I can do. Perhaps I verified that the question couldn't be answered."

"Bēhel says that *Records from the Oracle at Tuðá* is printed on nābimī. The answer can't just not be there."

"Everything is printed on nābimī."

"Again, it's *permanent*." Sīyas' eyes brightened. "Is something happening in the library? Something from higher-ups?"

"Nābimī isn't magic. Nobody can set it on fire. That doesn't make paper unbreakable," Tilōno said. "I can review the question. It's nice to know who actually asked." There was a small chance that it *wasn't* Bēhel — that this was the political quagmire Tilsa had alluded to. Tilōno wasn't sure that she believed Sīyas capable of that. She was more annoying than dangerous, and wanting to look good for one's elders was a transparent and disappointingly common motive.

"Really?"

"Just between us." *And Tilsa, and whoever else needs to be brought into this, like Tekīya.*

Sīyas' posture relaxed. She set her elbows on the table and leaned over her noodle bowl, pulling them into her mouth quickly. Tilōno followed suit. It was an Urang way of eating, and sitting across from Sīyas doing it felt like the most natural thing on Atara.

CHAPTER FOUR

Kalðī bounded towards the door and licked Tilōno's face when she arrived home, only two of ler sets of eyes open. Le stepped back and chittered excitedly.

Tilōno stroked Kalðī's auxiliary arms and picked lim up. The sensation of soft down was comforting after a hard day — and the feelings Sīyas stirred up needed to be caught before they moved any farther.

"I have a problem, Kalðī," she said.

The āyiki felt ler auxiliary arms along Tilōno's chest. As she walked through the hallway to the private comm booths, she grounded herself in Kalðī's steady breathing. Her own head felt light and airy, a helium balloon hardly tethered to the ground.

The co-housing comm booths were made of wood, with sound buffering panels the exact light gray one would ask for if one wanted them to show every stain. The relatively kempt one was in use, so Tilōno slipped into the one on the far right.

Tilōno set Kalðī down on the dark gray cushioned seating and slid the door closed. When she sat down, the āyiki curled up into a small ball and nuzzled ler beak against Tilōno's hip.

Someone was still logged in, personal communications about a very rough visiting marriage still open in all of the windows. Tilōno glanced towards the door. She heard no one coming. There had been no one in the hallway. It belonged to Mlēneingo ō Xeibam, one of the young professionals who had been in the building the longest. It felt wrong to see ler personal affairs spread out on the screen.

She logged out and went into her account. Sīyas had sent three messages since lunch, two of them about a singles' dance the following evening. Tilōno's family had a video request pending for sometime in the week. Tilōno had to schedule it.

Tekīya had left eight messages. She navigated to his profile and looked at his photograph, likely not updated since the spaceship grounding centuries earlier — nobody dressed like that anymore. Tekīya had poor organizational skills, but helping him with the āyiki and his other animal projects was not a civic appointment option.

The āyiki opened one set of its eyes, tracking Tilōno's manipulation of the video screen and cabled keyboard. She put in a vid request. Tekīya was probably not even there.

He responded eight minutes later, after Kalðī had started pacing and poking at stationary objects, auxiliary arms beating against cracks in the panels.

Kalðī stopped when Tekīya said, "Hello?"

"Hi."

"You waited a while to call me," Tekīya said, contorting his face into a pout. "How is the āyiki?"

"Everyone loves lim," Tilōno said. She pulled her knees to her chest, careful to keep her back from pressing against the booth's stained wall. "How is Owá?"

Tekīya shrugged and turned to glance at something off-screen. His eyes had a faraway sheen to them. Whoever it was, le only demanded his attention for seconds. "The town is gearing up for the election, very vicious. The candidates don't respect one other. My guess is that they will both be recalled. Oh — that percussion ensemble you like is performing next week, if you would like to visit."

She winced. Any adult could vote, but she couldn't vote for candidates in Owá while living in Maqá. Her family was backing the politician Tilōno didn't like, the one who wanted to relax regulations on how many hummod implants a person could have. Hūtong was the extreme limit, not having a real face. Tilōno would rather not see someone else like that. The opponent wanted to put pressure on the Atarahi Resources Bureau so it would redirect materials towards re-laying cable across the ocean.

"I may have time to visit soon," Tilōno said. "We're busy in the library."

"With what? You don't work past closing time."

"Someone has been razoring pages out of oracular books," she said, keeping her tone light and controlled.

Tekīya frowned. He scratched the nape of his neck. "Like, what kind of oracular books? The training manuals?"

"No. In the collection, the records from a specific oracular site. I was actually, um, wondering if you had access to them. Like other copies within the haribātna. Maybe one I could see." Her delivery sounded more awkward than she wanted, not like the confident child she had been on first seeing Tekīya. At least, she remembered being confident. "Can you help?"

Tekīya's face reddened, and he pursed his lips in anger. He didn't yell, unlike many times when she was a child and had asked him invasive questions about the haribātna. Kalðī put out an auxiliary limb and ran it down Tekīya's smooth, flat image.

Tilōno let go of her legs and moved into a cross-legged position. She snapped her fingers to call the āyiki. Kalðī climbed onto the seating beside her and nuzzled ler beak into her hand. She scratched ler chin.

"You are really calling me after over a week of saying nothing just to ask for a favor?" Tekīya asked scathingly.

"I've been busy."

Tekīya's nostrils flared. He shook his head. "You weren't busy *here* while studying for gender initiation and library science."

"I was just over the wall from you."

"And you're just over the network from me now. How is that any different, a physical versus a virtual wall?" Tekīya shouted and slammed his hand down on the table. His head whipped around towards someone off-camera, and he shook his head in ler direction.

Kalðī's limbs started to quiver anxiously. She stroked lim gently so le wouldn't start crying. "We've seen each other almost daily since I was nine."

"Don't you understand that?" Tekīya's breath came in raggedly. "I *miss* you because you're my best friend even though you are *so* young, and it's going to take me time to get used to not seeing you here. Just smiling, or cataloging, or organizing, or performing hāyiko temperament tests."

She shook her head. "This is about the oracles, Tekīya. It's not about any of that. Do you have them or don't you?"

Tekīya remained silent and staring, for a long time. The glassiness of his eyes hinted that his connection to the haribānōqi collective was active. Kalðī stopped quivering and settled down beside her, auxiliary arms slack. Sitting cross-legged stretched her inner thigh muscles uncomfortably. She hadn't stretched or exercised in days.

"There's a collection of oracular texts in Maqá, but they're not public," he said. "It's not the same type of oracular texts you have for public consumption in libraries. We have a slightly different access to oracles, and we record them in a different way. You could ask Luosa the next time she comes to consult the texts in your library. She goes every few weeks."

"What's the difference?"

Tekīya smiled and came back into himself. "How familiar are you with the spaceship grounding? The regulations, all of that?"

"Vaguely, from school. It's why we can't have most transmitting EM?" Most of the time, she saw the words *Regulation Certified* in glossy advertisements depicting human modifications, as all of it needed to pass the standard and not blanket the Heavens with noise.

"We perform divination to the Gods, primarily at the oracular site off the coast of East Southland. It's a private stretch of beach, Black Sands. On an archipelago, very remote. But you probably know that by now — ah. The texts are recorded and brought to Luosa, who leads the haribātna, and to Kaleḥ, who does the same for the qēssen." Tekīya's voice was softer, but his face hadn't lost its redness. "A lot of it deals with world issues ... like that."

The name *Luosa* sounded non-Sāqab. Tilōno doubted that Luosa had initiated into *she*. "And so you don't follow mortal societies at all?"

"I'm not an expert on oracular advice. I know it is pious to seek it out, but I've never considered myself an active devotee of any God. A conduit of Sasatū, perhaps, because I work with natural selection and genetics, but I'm told by others in the collective that that's reductive." Tekīya sighed. "You're eighteen. How many times have you personally sought out an oracle?"

"Once, when I wasn't sure if I wanted to do the womanhood

initiation. It was helpful. And birthdays, but that's routine." Her brow furrowed. Thinking about that made her anxious. There was no going back from an initiation decision once the mark was made on one's *qīne*, the soul's subtle garments, and the visible tattoos or piercings echoed that mark. "Rarely, I'd say."

"And working as a librarian apprentice in the Hall of Oracles, I imagine that *everything* seems as if it demands an oracular consultation. You have so many examples, so many materials around you. My opinion is that most people are fine using good sense. If you trust the God Kātiyo to bring good fortune, and if you balance tradition against the new, all will work out." Tekīya shook his head. He stared at a spot off-frame for a few seconds before looking back at her.

Tilōno pursed her lips together. "You're not going to help me because you don't believe in the uniqueness of oracles."

"I'm not going to help you because families razoring out one another's oracles from sacred library texts is a violation of sacred etiquette. I care about you and not helping you trip into harm's way. Have you opened my package yet?"

She nodded. "Yes." She hadn't. "Don't change the subject. Do you know any haribātna who lives near the National Library in Ural? They would have a copy of the oracular texts, too."

Tekīya shook his head and sighed. "I'm still angry with you."

"Why?"

"Were you not listening?" He sighed. "I won't jump bodies into some haribān in Ural and investigate the oracular texts, and that's a personal boundary. What I want from you is to treat me like you'd treat a friend, not a resource."

She clenched her jaw. *I have always treated you like a friend,* she thought. She had to figure out what was in that package. "Are we okay?"

Tekīya nodded. "Yes, we're fine."

"If you give me the details about the performance, I might have time to go if I take a train right from work." She smiled and leaned forward. Kalðī looked up at her with two sets of eyes and jumped down to paw at the door.

He nodded. "I'll message you. Does that mean you're taking off?"

Tilōno nodded. "There's a matchmaking dance tomorrow, and I'm going with a woman friend I made on the train. I have some other things to take care of tonight." Her cheeks felt hot, and her stomach started to do flips. It was ridiculous because Sīyas was irritating and unpleasant, but at least Sīyas had been messaging about things other than the oracle problem. "I've mostly been getting to know people here. Everyone's very different from home."

"Remember when the Maqáng get boastful: The name *Maqá* is from *Maqo Qaden*. They were the fifth settlement city, not the first. *Xe Qaden*, the first city, is in East Southland." He laughed uneasily and glanced offscreen again.

She shrugged. The haughtiness in her library colleagues came from their scholars' robes, not anything about Maqá. "I will."

They said their goodbyes. Tilōno resisted leaning back against the wall to decompress from the conversation. If Tekīya wouldn't help her, she would have to find some way out on her own.

Tilōno stood and walked to the door. Kalðī scampered into the hallway towards two other residents. Both dropped to their knees and fed Kalðī scraps of the fish jerky they were eating out of metal cups.

She smiled at them and passed by. Kalðī followed at a sluggish pace, greeting everyone. By the time le reached Tilōno's room, she'd already unwrapped Tekīya's gift and stood staring at it on the bed.

Seeing life extension formula in person filled her with terror.

The note that accompanied it was even worse. This was something that took approval to get — demonstrated attention to civic and cultural responsibilities being the key factor in an award of the formula. It never went to young people, especially not librarian initiates like her.

Her fingers shook as she lifted one of the tubes of amber-yellow fluid. It shone between her fingertips. The kit came with its own injection equipment. She read the doctor's statement and fumbled through her first injection, stomach churning with guilt.

Tekīya had already asked for the haribātna to bend the rules. He'd used the little influence he had to buy her time — because he cared about her, because he wanted her there — and she hadn't even needed to ask.

&❧

The dance took place in an ancient refurbished warehouse building that had once been used to build spaceships. The vast interior still bore some of the signage on the outer walls, now integrated into its fertility decor.

AI had given Tilōno eighteen male matches who were good candidates for fertilizing her eggs and giving her family its next generation. Dances like these were supposed to be icebreakers, and they often resulted in fertile, low-stress marriage contracts. Most used the same spermatozoa match to produce two children, and just over a third would do single-child marriage contracts. A fifth to a quarter would have a third child, which most countries still subsidized because the planet-wide population goal would not be reached for another millennium. Tilōno wasn't required to hew to the AI, unlike early Atarahi colonists, but she couldn't imagine not having it. It was overwhelming enough to consider that motherhood loomed over her.

A robotic attendant at the fertility shrine in the entryway alcove washed her hands and adorned her forehead with a fluorescent yellow dot. She bowed to the deities in the shrine and stepped aside to let a sselē be purified. The robot placed a pink dot on ler head, so le was compatible with Tilōno, but she did not recognize lim from ler matches list.

She went down a hallway, which echoed with dreamy music.

The hall opened into a large ballroom lit with bright, torch-hued lamps, its ceiling illumined by a field of pinprick starlight, transparent glass acting as a sound buffer for the mezzanine level. Water and fountains had created several dancing zones on the main floor. A staircase leading up to the mezzanine read QUIET CONVERSATION ZONE. On a stage at the far end of the building, an orchestral ensemble played traditional courtship music, complete with a singer and beat-heavy percussion. Most people on the lower level were dancing and joking with one another.

Tilōno checked her tablet against the people she saw. Tilōno had heard of people like her avoiding the male sex entirely by consummating the marriage in an asynchronous facility, but she would still need to pick the match here and make it clear that her contract would specify facility fertilization. She should have narrowed down her choices at home. The music, light, and crowds made it hard to think of anything but getting out.

The stairs up to the top lay beyond the noise-dampening panels and conversational seating. Two pink-dotted men were kissing in the alcove just before the stairs, ignoring the dance's purpose. She paused. Neither was a top AI match for her. When she reached the top of the stairs, she found their faces in the RSVP and flagged them as potential matches. One of them checked out as passable. She and the other were both carriers for a dangerous recessive trait, so the AI suggested against him. Tilōno complied.

The data would sync when she tethered in that night.

After she finished, she found Sīyas at a table at the far edge of the mezzanine close to the soundproofing. She hadn't made eye contact with Tilōno yet. Instead, Sīyas was watching the dancers in the mass of people below, pulsating in rings of women and men and sselētna. The yellow dot on Sīyas' forehead glistened even from that distance.

When she sat down across from Sīyas, she said, "I'm late because I had to feed the āyiki."

Sīyas nodded. "I don't mind." She shifted herself so she could meet Tilōno's eyes easily, but kept glancing down at the dancers. "Have you seen anyone you liked?"

Tilōno smiled and looked down at her fingers. "Not really. I didn't think much about the matchmaking until I realized I'd have to do it. It wasn't like the gender initiation. Everyone in the womanhood rituals actually wants to be there."

"It's only a four-year commitment for you," Sīyas said. "Why does it matter? It's just fertility."

Tilōno looked down at the dance floor. "One of my piblings had a marriage that turned into a romantic relationship. It was weird — as if le were playing at being one of *you*. Everyone teased lim about it. I have an aunt whose spouse became a stalker after it ended because he had a psychological attachment to the children. It happens, and it's a tragic part of being human, but I don't want to be in her situation."

"You're afraid of the contract." Sīyas smirked and tossed her hair to one side. She looked into Tilōno's eyes so intensely that the latter's belly started tightening. "Is that why you're wasting all of your time with a noblewoman you don't even like? Who asks you to do difficult things?"

"I wouldn't say that." Tilōno frowned.

Sīyas jutted her chin towards the floor. "I recognize a few faces.

That's why I'm up here — avoiding them and their inane banter. Our families don't like us coming here."

"They're also having marriages fixed like you?"

"Sort of. Being here is seen as low. For us, nobles have access to fertility fusion tech. I don't have to play around with *sperm* at all." The slang caught Tilōno off-guard. "That woman, you see her — there?" Sīyas jutted her chin towards someone dancing in a small crowd on the main level. "*She* is cruel. Yells a lot. She comes here toying often. Next month, she marries a sselē. Both nobility. They get the option of doing it naturally in person or at the facility, like you, or customizing according to their preferences. You don't have that option."

A sselē and two men glanced towards them from a small table a few meters away. Tilōno focused harder on Sīyas' face. "You're also here ... even though you're going to Ural."

Sīyas' gaze hardened. "I'm nothing like her. I'd rather find a commoner and have lim marry in. Female — woman, sselē, man, doesn't matter which lifeway le's taken oaths in. We'd have access to fertility treatment for ova fusion, just the same as if I'd married someone noble. Le'd join my family."

Tilōno shook her head and sucked her tongue against her teeth. "I wouldn't call the initiations *lifeways*. They're divine pacts."

"You're such a Midwayer." Sīyas shook her head. "What does *lifeway* mean there?"

"What it meant in Classical Atarahi. A social trend. Like when you look at a picture book illustrating professions and hobbies and personalities." Tilōno turned her head away. "I spoke a lot of Classical Atarahi growing up."

Sīyas clicked her tongue. "It refers to the deity initiation lineage here. Would you rather we spoke in the old language? It's stuffy in my mouth. You seriously went through the womanhood initiation and never heard the term used in that way."

Tilōno shook her head.

"Okay. Let's move on. Do you know why Ural struggles with its population?"

"I vaguely recall something." Tilōno barely knew anything about Ural and definitely nothing about its marriages.

"Your womanhood initiation lineage is for Inēs. You would only be able to do a marriage with a sselē, a manhood initiate of Yatotē, or a womanhood initiate of Hokiyokē, Inēs, or Hūto. Most male womanhood initiates look for a Mother consecrated to Tzōni, so you'll see maybe four or five in a class of twenty who have taken girlhood vows under a Mother. Yatotē lineages have a number of female manhood initiates. That's before the AI matcher gets involved. Your marriage pool is *terrible* in Ural." Sīyas rushed her thoughts out with barely a breath taken.

"We've only done the initiation rite together," Tilōno said. Her womanhood lineage was not marked public on her profile. "How do you know?"

"I was watching you during the initiation. We started together and were separated. The Mother who taught you is an officiant of Inēs." She paused. "Mine belonged to Tzōni."

"So I'm forbidden." Tilōno smiled.

"Only in Ural." Sīyas smiled back.

Tilōno's gaze traveled down Sīyas' shoulders to her wide arms, ending at the other woman's fingers. Sīyas took her hand. Tilōno didn't resist as Sīyas separated her fingers and worked hers in between. When she tried a clasp, it felt solid, electric.

Sīyas said, "I'm done looking at people I don't want. We should just do away with the entire distinction. Give fertility tech to everyone, right?"

Tilōno flinched. "That's seditious. You can't talk like that."

"I'm not an undercover PCA officer." Sīyas scowled and took

her hand away. "Let's talk about something else. Do you have anything about the oracles? It's okay if you don't."

Tilōno felt the absence of Sīyas' touch like an ache in her chest. "I need to talk to my boss, but le's been in administrative meetings most afternoons. It's hard to find time."

Sīyas looked down at Tilōno's outstretched hand. "Isn't le supposed to mentor you?"

"Yeah."

"Le's not doing a very good job of it, then." Sīyas fidgeted her chair closer. Its legs grated against the ground. "Look at your face. I'm not gonna hurt you."

Tilōno nodded. "Thanks." She raced through conversation topics. "What genres do you like? I mean with media, um, and all of that. I mean, um, tell me about you? If you're okay with that. It's fine if you don't want to answer, if you're trying to keep things distant. I'm fine—"

"Travel books. Virtual explorations of places only skilled climbers can go." Sīyas smirked. "We used to take the train out to one of Maqá's outer districts, where there's a satellite library with popular works. My piblings running for office would meet people while a few of us kids looked for adventure books. It's nothing like the National Library — far less somber of an institution. How about you?"

Tilōno shook her head. "I grew up reading a lot of software and hardware manuals. Animal research, too." It sounded too niche for conversation when she said it aloud. The room with Tekīya's notes — "and ephemera. I read a lot of ephemera and lab notebooks."

Sīyas nodded. "About that animal? The tame hāyiko."

"The āyiki. Kalðī, we're calling lim in the house," she said. "I didn't have many friends, so that's what I spent most of my time doing."

"Gods, not even temple dance?"

Tilōno lowered her gaze. "Not really." Her face burned, and she wondered what Sīyas would say. *You're too boring to be around*, perhaps. "I'm not very athletic."

Sīyas shook her head. "I'm athletic, but you need to be comfortable in your body to do music. It's not like that data-diving you do."

"What sports do you like?"

"Real diving, mostly. Water sports. I'd do hiking, but I have a problem with my knees and need to wait a few years before mod surgery. It's genetic." She glanced down at her legs and shrugged.

Tilōno nodded. "They taught me how to dive on Midway when I was four or five. Owá is landlocked, and pools aren't the same. My mom was sad about that."

"You have a weird look on your face," Sīyas said.

"Do I?"

"What's bothering you?" Sīyas shifted in her seat. She clutched Tilōno's hand tighter. The press of her body was too close.

Tilōno looked down. "The oracles. I'm not very good at not thinking about things that are bothering—"

Sīyas leaned in and kissed Tilōno before the latter had completely closed her mouth. She nearly bit Sīyas' lower lip before she relaxed and kissed back. It wasn't like what she imagined a kiss to be — something romantic done in intimate spaces, not at a matchmaker's dance while her belly writhed with anxiety.

The kiss ended just as Tilōno relaxed.

Sīyas pulled away and leaned back, the smirk still on her face. "You're really cerebral and just never get out of that skull, right?"

Tilōno felt lightheaded. She shook her head. "I get out plenty."

"Whatever happens with marriages, do you want to see each other? Date? It's okay if it's not the right time for you. I heard

Midway families get strange about dating while someone's supposed to have kids," Sīyas said.

Tilōno nodded. "Mine already let me move to Maqá, so it's not like I have to tell them. They know I'm making an effort at marriage by being here." She paused. "I think it's a fine idea."

Or she could marry you, Tilōno thought. It was unwelcome. She couldn't imagine leaving her family and joining Sīyas' for the rest of her life, of bearing noble children who would not know Midway. Even if they visited, those children would have surnames that Midwayers would greet with hostility.

She didn't know if she would like Sīyas in the long term. Here was a woman who had tried to bait her, who was intoxicatingly interesting, athletic, and capable. Tilōno wanted to rise in initiatory ranks, to be worthy of the life extension that now rushed in her system. Sīyas, unless she could become a cultural icon, would never have access to it.

And there were the issues of Tilōno's *other* piblings, the ones who had caused the rift in the family, and the perilous sacrifice her mother's generation had made in leaving. The sselētna within Tilōno's old surname, ō Nōtamsī, occupied key state positions. There was no telling what they'd do.

You're only eighteen, Tekīya would have said. *Have some fucking fun and leave me alone.* It was what he'd said when she was sixteen, fifteen, fourteen — and the young Tilōno had ignored it each time.

"A fine idea." Sīyas tilted her head to one side and clasped one of Tilōno's hands. "You're strange even if you're clever and a librarian."

Tilōno half-smiled. She was strange *because* she was a librarian and a scholar. Sīyas had never heard the chants, nor had she seen the sacred things in the chamber of darkness where the divinely-imbued objects and inks dwelled. There was the library everyone knew, and then there was the part of it where the Gods quickened forth.

"I have a question about oracles," Tilōno said. "How often do you give to the Tuðáng oracle? Tilsa says that family patrons pay per half-year."

Sīyas sucked her lips together and raised her eyebrows, creasing her delicate forehead. "Really? You still want to talk about libraries and books?" She let go of Tilōno's hand.

So Sīyas didn't know. "Not really. I just wanted—"

"Those are the elders, the ones who figure that stuff out. Bēhel would know," Sīyas murmured. She shook her head and said in a bemused tone, "You don't owe me anything because I kissed you. It's not transactional."

Tilōno didn't understand Sīyas' waffling — the question from earlier in their conversation juxtaposed against this stubborn unwillingness to talk suddenly. They couldn't just relax into romance when nābimī pages were missing. She reached for Sīyas' hands and clasped them. There was no script for how to navigate a romance before marriage, only after it ended. She drew Sīyas close and kissed her again — once on the forehead, then on the lips again. This kiss felt softer, more natural.

"Don't give me the answer over the Registry," Tilōno whispered. "I promise I won't talk about it for the rest of tonight."

Sīyas squeezed Tilōno's hands and rested her forehead against hers. There was a lot trapped in Tilōno's mind now, ricocheting around alongside the subject headings and questions about oracles. She dreaded asking if this meant they were going steady now.

Nothing about Sīyas was steady.

᠖᠉

That night, Kalōī lay curled at Tilōno's feet while she stared sleeplessly at the vacant ceiling.

There were tonics in the all-night dispensaries, and a robot could bring her one, but she wouldn't ask. The weight of Sīyas' lips against hers and the dismissiveness about Tilōno's attempts to solve ō Ćedīsam's oracle problem still buzzed inside of her skull. Now that she was home, she was angry, too. Mixing romance with serious matters left her all confused. Had Sīyas jumped at the chance to ask Tilōno because she wanted to see her again? What if it was all transactional and Tilōno was infatuated, as everyone told her young people often were? She had always thought herself immune to it, even though she sometimes glanced at others' curves and thought about kissing them. The intensity of this was different, uncomfortable.

In the long hours of night before daybreak turned the day-count forward, she decided to go for a walk with Kalōī.

She took a cord from one of her robes and fastened a loose harness around lim — Kalōī could breathe and move, but would not wander. Nighttime predators could come this far into cities from the wilds beyond. Even at this late hour, trains still ran, so they could always run for a transit shelter.

Kalōī squirmed while Tilōno worked. Le wouldn't follow her on the lead. She carried lim down the stairs, through the silent common areas, and out the front door.

The stars burned brilliantly. The Giant was ascendant in the northern hemisphere at this time of year, a fat pinprick that never wobbled like the stars. Mntaka was still visible at the other orbital Lagrange point, very small and just as steady. Atara followed both Mntaka and the Giant in roughly the same orbit. Stable planetary systems like this were rare, and ones in this configuration even rarer. Every place humans looked up at the stars was blessed. All stable waypoints for life were blessed, breathed into beings by Gods whom Tilōno could not even name.

She walked with Kalðī in her arms until le struggled free. Tilōno let the āyiki wander on the lead as le sniffed the unfamiliar leaf-shedder trees and shivered in the cold night. When le came back to Tilōno, the pads of ler paws were cold, and ler sensory limbs had drawn close around ler body, their knobs jangling in time with the cadence of ler feet.

Tilōno carried lim for another kilometer and let lim down just outside of the Maqáng oracular complex, sacred to the Gods Kātiyo and Unān. The temple precinct's outer wall showed both deites in frieze after frieze — Unān painted dark and studded with stars, Kātiyo shrouded in a gold and saffron-colored cloak that almost glowed in the pale red lamplight. Unān and Kātiyo shared a temple because Kātiyo was the Fortune-Giver, Le of Plenty, and Unān was the Hunter of Hours, sometimes depicted as a man, a woman, or a sselē, sometimes bearing children, sometimes siring them.

The *Proceedings of the Oracular Seat of Maqáng* came to the Hall of Oracles every two months. It contained fifty days of utterances and painstakingly annotated oracular interpretations for the benefit of the state and the querent who came. It was not like the regional centers where people asked for the identity of laundry thieves or what to name their children.

She could make a query if she had the money for offerings, and no one would know until the next *Proceedings* release that she had come here.

Tilōno had no tablet with her and couldn't check the price. It was also late, long past the queueing hour, so it would have to wait until tomorrow. She walked along the wall. Kalðī sniffed along the ground, often pulling the leash hard.

During the day, the shrine sites along the outer wall would have been filled with people, including divination-by-lots panhandlers and itinerant philosophers attempting at finding a following. Tonight, there was only the offering vending machine, its marquee advertising the seasonal specials, and the watchful silence of the small statues in each nook.

She held Kalðī's lead close while she examined the offering options. There were small, biodegradable flasks of nut milks and incenses of every kind and color. No dried cakes, though, which her family burned in their home's offering shrines and in Midway expatriate-friendly temples. Some of the incense here was powdered. Tilōno picked a stick incense that promised to smell like summer and the tropics.

The offering flame had powered down for the night. She relit it and gave the two long sticks of incense to the Gods, all the while feeling the silence of the city at her back. Kalðī chittered as le fought the lead.

She wrote her petition out in the women's script on a piece of paper and burned it on the flame between the incense holders. It was a simple prayer because Tilōno didn't know what to say. "Please help me find the information on those missing pages," she said solemnly, "and punish with severity the one who defiled pages from the Hall of Oracles, where your archived utterances wait patiently for interpreters."

A lone passenger transit train click-clacked down the central lane in the middle of the street behind them, bound for neighborhoods from the late-night entertainment centers. Kalðī stopped chittering.

The incense didn't quite smell like summer. It did not smell like the tropics at all.

She stepped away from the shrine without turning her back to it and continued leading Kalðī along the wall. Soon after, she picked the āyiki up and held lim in her arms, regaining feeling in her fingers from Kalðī's body heat. Traditional paper *burned*.

Nābimī paper required temperatures only reached in the special chambers that melted nābimī so it could be made into new texts. Nābimī paper had a scent like stone and old clay, like the walls of an old temple complex in the high-summer season. Both would stand the test of time.

Kalðī struggled down. Tilōno stopped to study the wall beside them. It depicted Unān trapped in a coiled jar at the heartpoint of the universe at the beginning of time before le learned how to hunt, weave, and dance. The jar had strange geometries barely renderable in the stonework. Unān stretched limself in all directions, and the jar exploded. Other stories of the Gods gave additional perspectives, but Unān was the platform on which all of those stories happened, a being that was everything, coiled and extended, dimensioned and dimensionless. The shards of the jar had become other, darker things.

The universe could not hide Unān or that dance.

"There's probably some trace I just didn't see," she murmured.

There were shards of that jar.

There were pages bereft of the books that once held them. Even if manually shredded, a bot could piece them together again. There was definitely no diamond-bladed blender in the Hall of Oracles.

They started walking again and went as far as the pedestrian bridge over the Amaí River, joined by a few late-night wanderers. They kept to themselves, which she preferred.

Tilōno stopped at the bridge's midpoint. She looked down over the black, meandering water as it flowed towards the inlet and Maqá Bay. The river here was wide, with many tributaries.

Before grogginess overtook her, she led Kalðī back home. Kalðī walked on the lead sometimes, she held lim at other times, and both were exhausted by the time they arrived at the house.

She didn't remember her dreams, just that they were

shrouded, as if she was seeing everything through a layer of nābimī.

⤫

Tilsa's office remained dark all the next afternoon. Hāyin and Hūtong spoke softly to each other in their workroom, and their voices barely carried beyond the door. Tilōno yearned for the moment when she could ask Tilsa about the oracular texts.

The reading room was busy, filled with users doing specialized projects. A Mother of the Rites of Womanhood sat at a table poring over oracles to find evidence that her parents had lied about something important in the family history. A group of young teenagers needed to consult the Wartime Oracles. Each volume was available in two copies, but only one of them was a use copy. She spent most of her time hovering over a noble sselē perusing family-specific oracular advice from the past twenty years to discern if the sites they patronized showed any particular pattern to the divine utterances. Accompanying lim were two younger sselētna and a girl only slightly younger than Tilōno, with no initiatory markings to indicate that le'd crossed over into womanhood yet. Luosa was reading alone. She did not engage much with Tilōno or ask any questions. Tilōno was too afraid to speak to her.

The staff door opened. Tilōno looked up. It was half an hour before closing time and an hour and a half before she would go home. Tilsa nodded somberly at Tilōno, unlocked ler office, and closed the door.

The teenagers left first, followed by the Mother. Tilōno opened the door for her departure and kept her gaze lowered. She still hadn't memorized all of the ways she was supposed to treat older women — those who had performed initiatory duties, especially the Mothers who taught girls how to be women and chaperoned them during the initiation. She was nearly certain that she'd used the wrong honorific pronoun for the Mother at least once and that she'd forgotten a hand greeting.

The noble and ler attendants stayed until fifteen minutes before closing time. As soon as they left, Tilōno gathered their materials and checked the books to ensure that nothing had happened to them. No cuts. No marks.

Luosa lingered until the very moment of closing. When Tilōno moved to escort her out, Luosa raised a hand and shook her head. The books she left were meticulously stacked. It would be easy to reshelve everything.

She left the tables for the robots to clean up and walked to Tilsa's door.

She knocked with her fingertips and waited.

"Ussēta Tilōno," Tilsa said as le opened the door.

"Director Ussēta Tilsa," Tilōno responded, lowering her gaze. She was so tired that she held the yawn in and let her nostrils flare out. "Is it appropriate for me to be here?"

Tilsa nodded. "Come in."

She closed the door behind herself and looked around the room. "Have you considered the stolen pages?"

"Not really. I've been in presentations all day about the new AI upgrades." Tilsa pressed ler lips together, then let out a sigh. A notification symbol strobed puffy and red on ler computer screen. "They won't have much of an impact on us. There was a quality control issue where AI was attempting to answer questions more appropriate for human intervention."

"How bad was it?"

"The Library Council is paying journalists not to talk until the upgrades happen and they can see that we have fixed this," Tilsa said. Le sighed. "The *paying journalists* part is not our idea. The haribātna and qēssen sent emissaries to tell us that we had to do it."

It would look bad for a library to lose control over its regional AI programs, and unlike before the war and the recent catastrophic data cable failures, there was nothing apart from the local AI infrastructure. One couldn't just use a library AI on another continent.

She said, "But the pages?"

"What about them?"

"What are your plans with them?"

Tilsa looked down at the locked cabinet thoughtfully. "To keep them here. You closed the question in the system, correct?"

Tilōno nodded vigorously.

Tilsa looked up at her and said, "Do you remember what I said about them? That there's no clear way to escalate?"

"Right. May I stay in your office and look at them again? I promise I'll be quiet."

Tilsa shrugged and opened the cabinets. "We have forty-five minutes before we leave." Le returned ler attention to the computer screen.

She brought the texts out and arranged them on a wooden table in the corner of the room. It was long and narrow, barely deep enough to hold more than a single volume, so she laid them out one by one in a line. The warped, old surface held the memory of staining dark drinks and beverage perspiration. It seemed disrespectful to place sacred things on it.

The *Records* looked the same as before. She had gone over them in detail. This time, she pulled out her tablet and pored over the floor for a stray data cable connector. There was one against the wall, barely within reach. She looked at the volume-level metadata. The volumes never indicated which families funded them, but linked to the data profile for each temple. Tilōno went to one of the oracular site's pages and scrolled through. Anyone could easily make a donation or request an oracular reading — even via proxy — but there was no public registry.

"Do you remember what I said about digital traces?" Tilsa said abruptly.

Tilōno turned around. "Right. I'm not doing much."

"It'll still show in the audit trails."

"But who has privileges for that?"

Tilsa shook ler head. "Administrators like me. Considering the circumstances of the vandalism, you need to be careful about this."

"How am I going to figure this out if I can't use the network?"

"There are methods," Tilsa said. "Higher-level initiates have access to them. Processes in the House of Ink, which—"

"Doesn't that go back to the original problem? If we have to be careful about the vandalism, how can someone be trusted to talk to the Gods of the Inner House of Books?" Tilōno knew that she'd overstepped when she saw Tilsa's face — eyes hard, cheeks flushed.

The sselē only stared at her. She felt the withering shame deep down in her gut. It was wrong to call out those who had seen higher mysteries. Tilsa's face was marked with them, and hers wasn't. Initiate-level rituals did not call the power of Gods from the cold spaces of reality. Advanced rituals did.

Tilōno disconnected her tablet and put her hands on her hips. Tilsa shrugged and looked back down at ler own work.

She couldn't expect ler help. There was very little Tilōno could do without access to the data stream. Even with it, she hadn't told Sīyas just how much was missing. The older pages might not all be centered on ō Ćedīsam, and she didn't want to worry Sīyas unless she could confirm it. Accessing financial records would require police intervention or a portal into the temple itself. Or the haribātna. Tekīya could easily locate the information. He and the others had clearance.

Sīyas still hadn't gone to Bēhel and probably wouldn't unless Tilōno revealed the true extent of the theft.

You won't know unless you try to ask him, she thought. *It's simple information. You just need to know which noble families donated in each half-year.*

But he hadn't given her access to the things missing within those pages. She doubted he'd assist with this even if it was easy and he'd never even have to leave home.

Oracles helped the nobility decide whom they should marry, when they should run for office, and whether they should keep silent — in the vaguest of terms, with advice that contradicted itself season after season. Most of the time, what the oracles said required skilled knowledge.

Anyone who needed more detailed interpretation would consult with religious specialists.

The noble sselē had brought pen and paper to take notes, with an entourage of family. Le'd used respectful grammar for one of the others in ler party, a long-haired sselē with many tattoos and piercings. Le had obviously been an officiant of Sasatū. Officiants of Sasatū often interpreted oracles simply because devoting oneself to a trickster God, the divine younger sibling of Kātiyo, a deity who could pave the road of chance the way le wanted, was auspicious for brainstorming responses to them.

Since the books themselves never left the library, anyone who wanted to interpret texts needed to bring the religious officiants unless they stole the texts. An unscrupulous officiant might not report a thief if paid enough money, and there were plenty of corrupt holy hucksters hiding among the sincere devotees of a God.

Tilsa removed ler ID card from the screen. It instantly went into sleep mode. Tilōno cleared her throat and said, "May I work in here for a few more minutes? I'm nearly done."

Tilsa's facial expression said, *That is a waste of time.* Aloud, le said, "The door will automatically lock behind you, and you cannot access any of my files with your ID card."

"I know that."

"Good."

She smiled. Tilsa didn't smile back, but le was her superior, not her friend. "Will the panel lock when I replace them?"

"Yes."

"Okay."

Tilsa crossed to a closet and took out ler coat, a beautifully-patterned garment that matched the tattoos on the backs of ler hands and just below ler lips. It was some kind of family pattern. There were books, scrolls, and abstract depictions of the data stream woven into it. *Librarian dynasty*, Tilōno thought. *This is how they mark themselves.*

After Tilsa left, Tilōno fought her instinct to connect the data cable again. Instead, she started reading the volumes' front matter, comments from an oracle's handler. This oracle had died in 4298 at the age of thirty-seven, burned out during a session that had given her massive internal bleeding and frostbite. The eulogy was heart-wrenching. Tilōno knew no one who wanted to become an oracle, but the Gods chose, and their humans adapted to the office or died.

Muffled footsteps from the reading room drew her out of the text. She looked up from the work. They stopped. All she could hear were the chittering robots in the stacks. The hum of machinery said that the night program had started. Only AI worked at night.

It was later than she wanted. The other professionals could feed Kalðī, but she would need to take lim out eventually.

Tilōno packed up and locked the cabinet. She left Tilsa's office and went to the librarian cubby outside to pick up her own coat and bag.

There were more footsteps from in the stacks. Tilōno looked beyond the reading room. One of the glass doors was open. A rustling noise came from inside.

She shrank back into the locker nook, not even daring to peek out.

When the person passed by, she saw ler shadow against the wall. It was hard to tell anything beyond that le wore a coat — like everyone else at this time of year. Tilōno waited until le'd almost reached the public exit before deciding to follow.

She didn't catch the door before it closed, but counted to fifteen and slowly turned the handle so it would make as little noise as possible. The figure walked through the public hallway as if le belonged. Le turned a corner. Tilōno crept into the hallway. When a board creaked, she froze.

Footfalls as if running. She squeezed her eyes shut. *Damn it,* she thought. *May the Gods break this person's feet and cause lim to fall.*

She turned the corner. The person had gone down any of several corridors far beyond her, all ultimately destined for the public reading room and the street. It would be faster to race back to the staff entrance.

Tilōno ran back to the Hall of Oracles and tried her ID in the door. It wouldn't work. She cursed under her breath — her ID wasn't authorized for night use in restricted collections, unlike Tilsa's. She had to go through the main staff tunnel.

She crossed to the exit and went down the library steps. The early evening crowd on the sidewalks was all home-bound, and there were so many people with coats. The main door of the library opened. Someone in a hooded coat walked fast down the stairs. In front of the library, the last commuter-schedule surface train lingered while scholars, librarians, and other professionals piled in.

Tilōno broke out running. There was commotion on the train, what looked like a host of scholars attempting to fit themselves around a child with a mobility apparatus, one of them being rude about it.

The person reached the train ahead of Tilōno. Le pressed limself in. It wasn't possible to see ler face, but the hood had fallen away in the dash, and ler piercings glinted in the train car's lights. Dangling earrings swayed from the left ear, and le hadn't switched to cold-weather, matte-finish adornments yet. Le turned slightly. There was less in the right ear. This *lim* was almost certainly missing an earring.

The train door closed. The person kept ler back to Tilōno. Le probably hadn't even seen her, even though le must have known *who* had followed lim given that she hadn't left. The first thing Tilōno would have done on a night like that would be to check if a staff cubby still looked full.

The train started moving.

She walked along the pedestrian side of the track in its wake, but turned away from Scholars' Walk to take the district rail terminal home. Her heart thudded in her ears.

Tilōno passed a theater just letting in ticketed attendees, a holographic garden, and commercial stores. There was a tether bar up ahead. Tilōno wondered if she should call Sīyas, maybe give her an update on what she'd discovered — or who she hadn't seen.

But no. Sīyas was confusing. Tilōno was tired, she hadn't slept, and she now needed to be at work early to check for earrings on the ground and hope that one of the robots hadn't reported it to lost and found yet.

It was probably bigger than ō Ćedīsam if someone was still entering the stacks like that to take things.

She had to call Tekīya.

δ♦

Tilōno made a request for a call via the Registry. Tekīya responded almost immediately with a time — long after dinner, about when Tilōno anticipated going to bed.

It was annoying to stay up so late. She was too useless and jittery to do anything but wait, stroke Kalðī, and listen to the scattershot conversations among the other professionals in the main common room. She couldn't even watch or read something out of fear that she might fall asleep. VR was a bad idea when tired.

At the scheduled time, she went into one of the cleaner comm booths and dialed. Tekīya picked up swiftly from a room within the haribānōqi house. Some of her housemates played a karaoke game in the common room, only half of them singing in the same key as the music. The sound carried into the hallway, and the soundproofing in her booth wasn't great. Tekīya's background noise was only ambient room tone, most of it filtered out. The haribātna hardly spoke aloud on their own, and from what Tilōno understood, they all viewed verbal conversations as some kind of mental chore. The only time they voluntarily spoke aloud around themselves was during prayer or song.

Tekīya was different, she liked to think.

He greeted her with a swift, curt smile and said, "I am still not going into that body as your glorified research assistant."

She nodded. Kalðī felt towards Tekīya's face on the screen, and Tilōno held lim back. "That's not the precise question I wanted to ask." She withheld that she'd essentially done a research assistantship for *him* since she was a child. "Many of the haribātna have access to financial data?"

"A few in the complex," Tekīya said guardedly, the frown on his face deepening. "What is *this* about?"

"I want to know which noble families supported the Tuðáng oracle and by how much each half-year for the past ten years. It shouldn't be a big data set." She narrowed her eyes. "You won't have to go into someone else's body."

Tekīya shook his head. His jaw clenched, but he didn't yell at her. Instead, he let out a heavy sigh. His pale skin flushed with anger. It was strange to see him holding himself back. "We haribātna dance among bodies all the time. It's not about that. Someone would say *yes* even to eccentric Tekīya."

"Why are you saying no, then?"

"Everything I said last time. I don't want my access to information to come between our friendship, and I can't say it much clearer than that," he said sharply. "What do you even think you'd get out of it?"

Tilōno hesitated. She pulled Kalðī back towards herself and stroked at the patterns of ler fur, idly staring at Tekīya. If she were among the haribātna, she could know his feelings instantly. As it was, she could barely control the tumult boiling in her belly and the certainty that this entire situation was damaging their rapport. "I want to make a simple dataset that just lists the noble families in descending order of sponsorship at the Tuðáng oracle, no monetary values necessary, and a list of the other oracles they support financially. I don't need any specific data about those yet. I'm going to cross it against the volumes we have so I can verify whose information is missing, and I'll progress from there. Sīyas, a woman I met on the train, contacted me and asked me about the reference question. It was from her family, ō Ćedīsam, but she doesn't know just how much is missing. Probably forty, maybe fifty pages." She paused. "I don't think whoever it is will stop at Tuðáng. There was someone in the stacks tonight who shouldn't have been. I didn't see what le did. Maybe someone else's texts are missing. But with family names, I could then *hopefully* pull which oracles the missing ones support and find out if any other texts are missing. Assess the scope. Does that sound like a good research question?"

Tekīya's eyes narrowed as she spoke, and his look of contempt unsettled her to her core. He'd never looked at her like that before.

"You know? You don't—" she started.

"I can see what I can do. Don't wait for me, if you're relying on it. You need another plan." His lips pursed together as if he were trying not to scream. She'd seen that expression before when he was speaking with the other haribātna in the Owáng mansion.

Tilōno had another message on the line, a bright purple bubble of women's script. *Tilōno? I haven't heard from you. Could you vid me? Can we meet?* It was from Sīyas. Her heart pounded. Now was not a good time. "Do you have any suggestions about another plan?"

Tekīya shook his head. "You are a library science graduate. Surely you read your subject matter well and have some inkling of another thing you could do. There are people among the haribātna initiated into those mysteries. Taḥas, a librarian in my complex, told me that you should be able to solve this on your own. Le's also saying that you're having a scope problem. Keep this simple. Nobody razors out nābimī without a lot of forethought."

"Tilsa won't even let me look things up online. Audits and intrigue."

"You can't limit yourself to your manager." Tekīya shook his head. "Do I allow Luosa to control what I do? No. If people were following you in the audit modules, I'd tell you even though that's not allowed."

Tilōno let go of Kalðī. Le jumped down onto the floor and scratched at the door. Tilōno shifted to let lim out and looked back at Tekīya on the screen. "What do you know about rituals of library science?"

"Enough to know that you haven't thought of everything. Nothing is private in the collective."

"Tilsa said there were options." She closed her eyes and tried to envision her library science textbooks, scrolling through pages and pages in her mind.

A Head Librarian could work rituals and petition the Triad for the good of the collections. Tilōno could read the less role-specific rituals as much as she wanted, but without instruction in library arcana, they would remain flat and lifeless if she performed them.

The religious officiants of library science might have the answers. She opened her eyes. "Does Taḥas think I should talk to an officiant? Maybe one who obviously isn't involved in political intrigue?"

"I am not your messenger, remember? You can find Taḥas' contact information in the Registry and contact lim yourself." Tekīya shifted in his chair and switched the cross of his legs.

"I know. Sorry."

Kalðī made a shuffling noise on the other side of the door. Another message popped up from Sīyas: *Tilōno? Maybe you're not here ...*

"I received the itinerary for next week," Tilōno said. "Everything is clear with work."

"That's good to know."

"I need to take another vid. Message me when you have something?"

Tekīya leaned back in his chair and smiled at her. "I'll send you a message if we locate it. Again, don't expect this to be fast. Goodbye, Midway child."

"Bye."

Tilōno hung up. She clicked on Sīyas' dialer while she opened the door for Kalðī. The āyiki now carried something in ler mouth, a piece of discarded meat from the communal kitchen. It was raw and probably not very sanitary. Tilōno sighed and pulled it out of ler mouth.

Sīyas answered immediately and said, "You're here!"

"I was talking to a friend. What do you want?" The other woman paused and blinked. The language was too informal, Tilōno realized, even if they were seeing each other now. "How are you?" Tilōno corrected herself.

The noblewoman smiled softly and said, "I wanted to see your face. Been thinking about you."

Tilōno tried to think up a reply. "I've been thinking about you, too." It wasn't exactly a lie.

"There's a holographic garden near you open late tonight. Do you want to go? How early do you have to be up for work?"

"Early," Tilōno said. "I need to sleep. Didn't have much last night."

"Oh." Sīyas frowned. "Well, some friends and I will be there, anyway — I was hoping to introduce you. Will you let me know if you change your mind?"

Tilōno nodded. They said goodbye, and she hung up and logged out. She felt like shit, but there wasn't anything she could do about her restlessness or the weight of oracular infinity upon her mind. She yanked her tablet from its tether and let herself and Kalðī out. They walked past everyone enjoying themselves and up the stairs. She felt acutely aware of their eyes on her.

CHAPTER FIVE

Tilōno had only slept for a few hours when Kalðī awoke her by pressing ler beak against her face, tongue clicking, facial spines taut. A small *thunk* against the wall shifted her attention to the wall with windows. At the fifth thunk, she pushed Kalðī aside and slipped from the bed to look out.

Tilsa stood on the ground below in a coat, pale face emerging from the soft hood lining like a specter floating in nothingness.

Her boss crouched down for another pebble and threw it. This one hit the window and bounced away, making no impression on the glass.

She couldn't find the window's latch. It was a double-sealed contraption meant for the hard winters of the Northland continent, which allowed precious winter daylight in while sealing the building against drafts, and the panes generated electricity to offset the wind and tidal farms nearby. The controls were complicated. She dressed quickly — in simple pants, a shirt, and socks.

Kalǒī followed her to the door, where she put on her shoes and coat to go meet Tilsa, and le nearly tripped her as they went outside. She walked around the corner of the building. It was far colder than the night before. The two nearly spherical moons overhead glistened in the light, with at least three or four other tiny companion rocks also visible in the sky near the horizon.

"What are you doing here?" she murmured, arms pulled tight to her chest. "Do you know what hour it is?"

She'd had four hours of sleep, but the fatigue still tugged at her. Atara rotated on its axis nearly as slowly as Ameisa, a factoid she'd memorized despite how little it mattered. Four hours was a decent amount of time.

Her boss said, "What's that animal?" Le smiled, the edges of ler lips strained.

"Kalǒī, an āyiki. It's like a hāyiko, but tame. I have a friend who domesticated them," she said softly, "for companionship."

"Strange hobby."

"He's my haribān friend. How do you know where I live?"

Tilsa shrugged. "Your personnel file. I don't live far from you, just a few blocks." Le kept ler voice low. "I usually take a walk in the middle of the night. My younger child has nightmares, and I go out after I put lim back to bed."

"But why are you here?"

"You went to the Maqáng oracular site last night." Tilsa shrugged, hands snuggled inside of ler coat pockets. "I was up on the boulevard. Not many young women have bright coats in Maqá, especially green ones."

Tilōno looked down at her coat. She frowned up at Tilsa. Her boss had dressed for the outdoors, not just a midnight outing — spacers still in many of ler piercing holes. Kalǒī approached Tilsa, stretching ler sensory limbs forward, and touched the sselē's legs.

The thin fabric of her pants let in the icy breeze as it moved across the ground cover, a reminder that winter was coming fast. She said, "I did."

Tilsa nodded. "Was it about the missing oracular texts?"

"Ultimately." Saying *yes* would have made it sound as if Tilōno had a plan. "Are you the one who stole them?"

The words escaped her lips before she had time to think them through. Here was her boss, an important sselē thrust into the position of mentoring a new librarian, someone whom the gossip said had been unprepared for the position when le'd moved into it. Here was *she*, a librarian apprentice who still lived in young professionals housing instead of with family or in maternity cohort housing.

Tilsa looked at Tilōno's barely-covered feet. "I still think it's politically wise not to investigate."

"You wouldn't be here in the middle of the night if that were true."

"Correct," Tilsa said. Le jutted ler chin towards Tilōno's shoes. "Those won't do for where we need to go."

Tilōno took in a deep breath. "Director Ussēta Tilsa, how does it look for you to not care about pages' disappearance and to suddenly look for the subordinate who discovered them in the middle of the night? Would you walk somewhere with that director?"

Tilsa smiled. "Perhaps not. Let me put it this way: We're only a few generations out from the war, and we have had families from among the commoners and the nobility exiled to a variety of islands and other nation-states, sometimes even killed. What do you *think* will happen if this isn't settled discreetly? We would need to inform the families with compromised data either way, but going through the Head Librarian will be messy. Someone could assassinate either or both of us before we solve the problem."

"Who do you think stole them?"

"It's either someone who wants to prevent ō Ćedīsam from accessing oracles relevant to those families — or it's something larger and systemic, and we've only scratched the surface." Tilsa clicked ler tongue and shook ler head. "I've worked in the collection long enough to know that important people use it regularly. When they trust you, and when you come from a family like ō Naítam that has worked in libraries for centuries, they will ask things that I do not care even to repeat in the darkness outside of a newly-fabricated apartment."

"And why are you coming to me now?"

"Because depending on what the passages said, my judgment could sway one way or the other." Le looked Tilōno up and down. The condescending smile was unbearable. "Go change your shoes and come back outside, Ussēta Tilōno."

They had an eternity of hours before sunrise, and the library wouldn't open to the public until an hour afterward. Tilōno's feet twitched back towards her front door. She didn't move. "Where are we going that I need better shoes?"

Tilsa blinked slowly. "Temple-bound rituals are not the only way to get this information. I know a necrobibliomancer. We'll take Ayō's Cradle to the end of the line and go into the woods. Le lives just beyond the city's edge."

Tilōno's heart hammered. She felt like she might get dizzy. "What's actually the difference between a necrobibliomancer and a normal bibliomancer? Beyond that it's fraught." *Normal* bibliomancy could already mean one of three things: the rituals practiced by advanced librarians for the Triad, the use of whole books and cut-out passages from books in some kinds of street divination; or magical practices like in the *Ag Vuxōqi Nivssē ag*

Natawāmu.

"A bibliomancer would perform divination or make charms for you to dive deeper into the stream of data, if you wished, or le'd devise incantations to navigate you to the correct information. A necrobibliomancer specializes in the magical reconstruction of texts that are missing, lost, or destroyed." Tilsa grimaced. "That activity is not precisely legal when performed outside of a library. One needs approval. There is paperwork. Le lives beyond city limits, and there are loopholes that make doing this not precisely illegal, either, in ler case."

She gritted her teeth and nodded, then went back into the house. Kalðī followed just at her heels. She didn't want to go alone with Tilsa, and yet she couldn't endanger the pet entrusted to her care.

Tilōno didn't change immediately. Her first stop was in the kitchen at the knife drawer. If something went wrong or if Tilsa truly had stolen the texts and wanted to be rid of her, Tilōno would not become some Midway barely-adult who allowed herself to be duped and killed. She found a good, solid knife with a sheath in one of the drawers.

By the time Tilōno made her way back to Tilsa, she'd left Kalðī to wander the hallways alone. One of the other professionals would let lim into ler room, probably within the next fifteen minutes. People awoke at all sorts of hours as the darkness overtook Northland to amuse themselves between a first and second sleep. She usually slept through the night.

It seemed just as cold outside now with proper clothes as it had been before. The knife hardly bumped at all against Tilōno's thigh in the pocket where she'd placed it, and she almost wondered if she'd left it on the bed, too anxious about the idea of pulling it on a supervisor and higher-level initiate in the library mysteries — even though, in this specific context, Tilsa would be trying to kill her if le'd lied about the noble families and the necrobibliomancer.

Tilsa waited in the shadows of the trees, and she fell into step beside lim as they departed. Le didn't carry limself as Tilōno imagined a person capable of murder would, and as they walked along the train tracks waiting for one of the late-nighters to pass, Tilsa hovered over Tilōno like a parent.

"How do you know the necrobibliomancer?" she whispered after a long while, just as she'd resigned herself to the thought that they might have to walk all the way. "And does le know we're coming?"

Tilsa shrugged. "I left lim a message. Dēnasa. Ler name is Dēnasa." Le smiled slightly and glanced down the tracks. There wasn't a train in sight. "Dēnasa and I went to concerts together when we were younger. Le's a decade or two older than me, formerly a librarian in Tuðá. Particularly interested in esoterica, and then le went further with it than anyone thought proper."

"But le has a tether line so le can receive messages."

"It's the forest, not the middle of nowhere," Tilsa said. Le shook ler head. "Many people are willing to pay good money for a mystic like Dēnasa."

Tilōno closed her eyes. Something akin to a train rumbled in the far distance. "You used the word *mystic* and not *magician*."

"Dēnasa talks to Sanwū, Sasnē, and Sa. I don't know how else to explain it. It's like what oracles do." Tilsa grabbed Tilōno's hand tightly and pulled her back from the tracks, which whined with electricity as they prepared for the approaching train. "You'll have to see it for yourself. 'A God plays the oracle as wind plays through a flute,' as the saying goes."

They stopped walking and pressed a button to signal the train. It curved around a bend on the track and started to slow down. The train was only three cars at this hour of night, each of them half-empty. They boarded and sat a few seats behind a large group of costumed young adults talking loudly about a fantastical improv game while one of its members fixed a faulty VR generator on the floor.

The pallid lights gleamed on the bright gray seats, and the illumination obscured most details of the world outside. She slouched down in her seat and looked up at the ceiling, which advertised community events in neighborhoods she had never noticed on the maps. "Do you think the Gods wonder at the kinds of questions people ask oracles, though? Where to find their pillowcases and whether someone at a person's workplace hates lim."

Tilsa shook ler head. "I don't know. I just work in the collections. Whatever is recorded on those pages is meaningful to somebody. That's how oracles work." Le leaned back in ler chair, too, and sucked ler tongue against ler teeth. "I should tell you this. Dēnasa and I dated for a short time long-distance before I decided to go into the marriage pool and have children."

"Why did you wait?" She didn't ask about the age difference. Tilsa must have been eighteen or nineteen when they started dating. An eighteen-year-old with a thirty-something would be frowned upon by most families.

"Because I'm a sselē and my family let me. Also, while I wasn't studying to be a librarian, my friends and I were trying to break out as a pop band. It was secular stuff. We'd play in the restaurant circuits along the river, sometimes in the holographic garden entertainment," le said. "My grandparents would always say, *What is that Tilsa doing out so late every night?* My grandfather was the head of the library in Maqá then, and my other grandparent was at a high-level administrative position in the National Archives. Dēnasa liked our music. We kept going to concerts after the band broke up. I actually did two degree initiations during all of that, first as a librarian, then as an archivist. That's why I was placed in the Hall of Oracles. I was thinking of going into music librarianship. Nobody is appointed to the Hall of Oracles who actually wants to be there. It's better for security that way."

Tilōno thought back to the application she'd filled out online among all of the open apprenticeship positions. It hadn't been for a specific job — they applied for library studies, and the national system placed them after their final initiation. It was similar for professionals. "But no degree in music."

"No. But also, the applications would have shown my surname, and they prefer ō Naítam in high-profile collections, regrettably." Tilsa breathed in sharply and looked down the car at the group of young people. Even with the loud chatter all around, two or three of them had fallen asleep. "What we're about to do is weird, Usséta Tilōno, much stranger than anything you may have read in the *Ag Vuxōqi Nivssē ag Natawāmu*."

"Some of the people in library school did spells and petitions to prepare themselves for the data stream," Tilōno said with a shrug. "There would often be groups going for picnics that were not picnics towards sunset, even after the snow came."

"Did you go?"

"No." Tilōno half-smiled and turned her head towards lim. "My family is in medicine and engineering, and I've always known that meditation and direct prayer are better to steel the mind against the deep dive than magical charms. The latter seem a bit desperate, and how can desperate people go into the dark chamber where Sa waits in ink?"

Tilsa shook ler head. "Don't discount the charms. My family has done them for centuries."

"I'm the first in my family to go into library science."

Her boss had nothing to offer but a sigh. It was clear that a curtain had come down between them like the ones in the prefab home Tilōno's family still inhabited.

It could have been other things, too. Most people still asked Tilōno things about Midway that only people raised there would know. Tilōno remembered how to swim and to physically dive, not much else, and one prepared for physical diving the same way Tilōno prepared to enter a data stream chamber. It was all about staying calm and collected. As in traditional Midway diving, there were no tools to help someone, just the mind and breath control. It took discipline to go deep.

The loss of the final cable had severed Northland from Midway, where the best librarians dove into data. Now, Midway had its good information services. Northland had its own and a few connections to its minor islands. East and West Southland had tenuous connections to each other and to Quarterway Island. Midway was only connected to the data cables of the Greater Archipelago. Everything was tenuous. It would take a long time to catch all of the cable-cutter bots.

In Northland, her children would be severed from Midway culture just as Midway was severed from the data streams of the major continents.

"My family knows charms for traditional diving," she offered, "and the initiatory prayers for medical insights to the Gods of healing and medicine. What I've seen my mother do is not the same as the library things I have seen."

Tilsa shifted away from Tilōno and said, "The Information Triad are not the same Gods, so it would make sense that the rituals are different."

"I know." She cleared her throat. "Does it bother you? What I said?"

"A bit."

"Do you regret bringing me?"

Tilsa said nothing.

"You could have gone on your own without fetching me, right?"

"You're my mentee." Le drew air in through clenched teeth and breathed out sharply. "A mentee whom they assigned to me and whom I never would have chosen. Not because of anything about you. I just don't see myself in the same way that the decision-makers do."

She rolled her eyes and canted her head to the side. "You're angry that I never dabbled in esoterica. That's not the same as being a bad mentor." *They probably wanted you to relax a little and to get out of your bubble*, she thought. *If you've never interacted much with people who've never had a librarian in the family, what do you know?*

"I'm not angry."

The train came to a stop, and the improv gamers piled out. The ones who had fallen asleep lagged behind, duffels lurching and slipping along the floor as they hurried to the door. Their departure left Tilōno and Tilsa almost completely alone save for a few people reading books or interacting with their tablets. It was dead quiet.

It was not a good time to talk about hidden teachings or the magic that some librarians performed while they prepared to enter the walls of the houses of books.

∂♦

Tilsa and Tilōno detrained at the last stop. The neighborhood looked uncannily like the one from Tilōno's childhood — prefabricated houses, most so alike despite the efforts to engage with different architects that it would be impossible to tell homes apart without actually living here. It had the same layout, too, with wide open spaces, exercise paths, supply stores, and gardens.

The small shrines dotting the neighborhood were also new, most made of heavy-duty materials — as in Tilōno's neighborhood, whoever had thought through which Gods needed ones had obviously been a city planner. There were other shrines, scrap-made and almost as solid, to the Gods that the people had brought with them when they'd moved in.

They walked along the road without making offerings. She tried avoiding eye contact with the icons. Tilsa stared at the ground, and only when Tilōno asked about the distance did le speak.

"We're going about a kilometer into the forest."

"Okay," Tilōno said. She looked ahead at the darkness beyond. There wasn't enough moonlight tonight to light their way. "Do you have a flashlight?"

Tilsa shook ler head. "The path will be clear enough that we won't trip. If you need assistance, just stay behind me."

She didn't ask how often Tilsa came to this place that le knew how good the path was. The forest loomed ahead of them, choked with native Atarahi undergrowth and trees. It wasn't curated like the gardens in cities, nor was it as simple as Tekīya's wall. She couldn't imagine that any path through it would remain clear for long. The plants would thicken into any open places.

The broad sidewalks ended in a park, and beyond that, forest. Tilsa led her perpendicular to it until they reached a small gap where they could slip between the trees.

Kalðī wouldn't have been good here — too tame and too prone to running off. The forest at night had animals in it that made noises like low drumbeats and high, whistling choruses. Bioluminescent, cold-tolerant insects and predatory animals moved through the branches all around them. In the distance, something made rustling and cracking sounds as it snapped the bent wood from the trees.

Atarahi trees used several compounds in addition to chlorophyll, but in the darkness, all looked the same — shadows of their daytime glory. Their branches came out of their trunks like spines, twisting this way and that as they fought towards the canopy, where the rectangular, waxy leaves were out in full. Tilsa walked between them easily, but Tilōno's coat caught on everything in their way. At one point, she ended up on hands and knees, and le helped her up.

They came to a clearing, the sky still deep and starry over their heads. A circular building halfway between a tent and a permanent structure stood in front of them, too small to hold many people. Cables came out of the ground just before the building in the foreground and wormed their way into its fabric crevices. As they approached, she realized with horror that what stood in front of them was entirely made of synthetic fur and skin. Beyond this structure lay a circular brick building from which smoke came, and light flickered in that building's open doorway.

Tilsa rapped ler fingers against the outer wall, not squeamish at all about touching it. Tilōno's gaze strayed to the larger building. This was not the kind of place she expected a necrobibliomancer to live.

The one who pulled back the tent door had graying hair in two large braids down ler back, the hair gathered in stages so it looked like a deep sea-creature's spine. Le'd already replaced ler piercings with nonmetallic, winter-ready ones, each of the prayer tassels looped so it wouldn't catch on heavy scarves or soft-lined coats.

Like Tilōno, le had the curved symmetrical lines spiraling up from the center of ler chin to just below the edges of ler lips and the lobe and daith piercings with prayers on them, along with a bridge piercing that marked lim as completing the first five years of ler ritual obligations, when they were mandatory instead of optional. Like Tilsa, le had reed-like curves coiling up ler chin on either side of the gender tattoos, so they had both studied some of the advanced mysteries of the Reed Goddesses. Le bore Southland-style manhood piercings in ler eyebrows and a more traditional manhood piercing on ler septum. Instead of the shield-piercing in ler lobe customary for millennia, le had a row of diamond and triangular designs across ler cheekbones, again like someone from Southland.

She was staring and aware that she was staring, so she looked away. Tilsa had used *le*, not *he* or *she*, to describe Dēnasa. There were no pronouns or verb forms that could capture that Dēnasa could use both *gotomis* and *nepma* without being awkward. Where did Dēnasa go inside of a home if le was barred from both the women's and men's sections by mutual exclusion? Le also bore the many markings of a librarian, someone at a very high level.

Tilsa gently nudged her aside and hugged Dēnasa. The two of them stood in the doorway for a long time before they separated, and Tilsa canted ler chin at Tilōno. "She's my librarian mentee, Tilōno ō Vōwusī, who discovered the problem I mentioned vaguely in the message. Tilōno, this is Dēnasa au Kaíram, Ussēta fu Nivssēkabī." *Esotericist-Scholar.*

She bowed her head at lim and went down on her knees in a half-prostration, something not required for people like the Head Librarian or Tilsa, but customary for those with esoteric skill. "It is a pleasure to meet you, Ussēta Nivssēkabī Dēnasa."

"You may stand," Dēnasa said. Le clicked ler tongue. "Tilsa, you never said that your mentee was so polite."

Tilōno rose to her feet. Red spread across Tilsa's face. Le said, "She is a welcome addition to the staff."

Tilōno had never been called *polite* before — often *rude* by

Tekīya, *too Demzang* by her mother. She said nothing.

Tilsa said, "Tilōno discovered missing pages in several volumes of the *Records from the Oracle at Tuðá*, and we need to know what they say."

Dēnasa nodded and looked Tilōno over. "How did you make lim listen to you?"

Tilōno shrugged and said, "I don't know."

"She's been very distracted by it and making offerings in the middle of the night at temples," Tilsa said, "and that's not good for her. I know that you think I'm too clean-cut to do magic against my family's best interests, but we have a clear reason to be here."

"Because you're interested in mentoring her. You would never have done this for someone coming in and crying in your office, and I know that because I've had people come to me after interacting with ō Naítam, and that is what they all say. You all love rules." Dēnasa's eyes narrowed.

Tilōno followed the discomfort in Tilsa's posture. It was no wonder that they'd broken up, that Tilsa had briefed her on their relationship before approaching this door. She'd seen passive aggressive exes interacting at temples throughout her childhood because most Midway Island expats went to the same ones and sat on the same boards and recreated in the same sacred parks and baths, and the population was too small to avoid the interpersonal drama.

But Tilsa had told her to come with *lim*, not alone. The Director of the Hall of Oracles could have told her to do this on her own. She cleared her throat and said, "We need to know what's happening in those texts because they were razored out of the books. It's nābimī paper, so none of the writing has been destroyed unless the thief has access to nābimī disposal mechanisms. And we can assume the texts are somewhere else."

"If one of the demimortal collectives razored them out for international security reasons, they would have been destroyed," Dēnasa said. "The haribātna and qēssen sometimes corrupt data or destroy it if they don't think it's regime-safe."

"What would that have to do with a family? The international regulations are all technology things, like EM bands and how to get a permit for an atmospheric or space plane. Who does divination about that?" Tilsa's tone was dismissive even if it was phrased as a question. Le rolled ler eyes and put ler hands on ler hips. "We'll assume a mortal unaffiliated with them took it. Ergo, the only time the texts would be *thoroughly destroyed* is if this was a state initiative. And I checked with a contact in the government late in the afternoon. There are no active movements against families right now."

"Well, it's good to know that nobody else is getting exiled." Dēnasa laughed. "Privileged assholes the lot of you."

Tilōno cleared her throat. "Look. Can you help us with the texts?"

"You know my fees, Tilsa."

"We want you to resurrect a page with the most pertinent and time-sensitive oracles. Something representative. Can you do that?"

Dēnasa gritted ler teeth and narrowed ler eyes. "Really, Tilsa."

Tilsa drew a small pouch out of ler pocket, embroidered with solar system patterns, and knelt down to place it on the doorstep. Le did not meet Dēnasa's eyes the entire time. Dēnasa waited until Tilsa had regained ler position beside Tilōno to pick up the pouch. It was likely appropriate for her to avert her eyes, too, but she needed to know what was inside. Dēnasa would have used the same digital credits as everyone else to buy what le needed to survive, and while she was far from an appraiser, it mattered that she knew how expensive this really was.

Dēnasa opened it into ler palm. Gold and semiprecious stones glittered in the light. It was a devotional necklace with ninety-nine beads, a figurine charm of the Goddess Bē in the anchor position. The ninety-nine beads stood for the ninety-nine traditional epithets of Bē, some known, some unknown. Tilōno had beads for the Triad. They were expensive because a religious specialist had to make them, pray over them, and give them to a person — several hours of someone's time. Tilōno's had cost a month's spending money beyond lodgings, saved up by her family during the first year of her library studies.

The esotericist clicked ler tongue and nodded in satisfaction. "You didn't just buy these."

"They're from my family's cache," Tilsa said, "for moments like these. This was used by Adīsa. You can see her mark of ownership on the back of the Goddess' icon. They're worth a lot in trade."

"So they are." Dēnasa nodded, inspecting the owner's mark. "Thank you."

She couldn't ask Tilsa if this was the standard price. *Le* knew the underground magical economy, not her, and perhaps a historical object was it. Adīsa was the librarian who reformed Atara's Registry metadata system right after the spaceships were grounded, and she was venerated as a heroine by students in many disciplines — library science, security, and beyond. The esotericists hawking amulets to students at the Grand Pavilion in Owá charged in-market credits, cheap enough to save up and buy after a few weeks without making too many sacrifices in other areas.

Dēnasa turned away from them and shut the tent flap behind lim. Tilōno caught Tilsa's eyes. Tilsa said, "We can go wait outside of the ritual space. Le'll be along."

They walked to a bench just outside of the circular brick building. "While le's busy, can you tell me how much this service costs?"

"It depends." Tilsa looked down and poked at the ground cover with one toe. "I still haven't completely convinced myself that le can do this."

Great, Tilōno thought. *This is just what I need. I wonder what Tekīya has.* "What do you mean?"

"The ritual is very strange." Tilsa folded ler hands in front of lim. Ler fingers twitched. "Very strange indeed. Dangerous."

Dēnasa emerged from ler hut and walked towards them. Ler ritual clothes bore no resemblance to what the esotericists wore in town. They looked almost like businesspeople, but Dēnasa wore a sleek, black robe star-patterned with inexpensive diamonds and gathered at the waist with a silver cord. It looked like it had been a bedsheet in its first incarnation.

Two ropes of prayer beads lay around ler neck, one to the Triad and one to the hidden Goddess who taught Sa, Sasnē, and Sanwū the secrets of diving into water like the ūyo animals along the shore in winter, the deity who gathered memories and experiences of people like animals preying on specific fish from among the masses beneath the waves.

In ler right hand, le carried a basket of wooden balls painted with symbols in various colors and combinations.

Le carried a libation vessel in ler other hand, which remained capped. As Dēnasa approached, Tilōno caught the generalities of its design, a lattice-like netting of the universe common in many of the older paintings of Gods, who bore the hexagonal webbed design like tattoos on their hands, feet, mouths, ears, and around their eyes. It had fallen into disuse within the past few centuries as deities had taken on tattooing that looked more natural and human.

Dēnasa opened the wooden door with ler elbow and went inside.

Tilsa stood, and so did Tilōno. When Dēnasa emerged a few minutes later, le lit the torches on either side of the door and set a stick of aromatic herbs burning. Tilsa spread ler arms out wide for the cleansing, and so did Tilōno. The potency of the herbs made her head spin. The blend may have contained ruby-colored ćas, a painkiller and relaxant smoked by some older people, in which case she knew she couldn't trust the slow numbing sensation of contentment as it dissipated into her.

Next, Dēnasa bound their mouths with black cloth. They slipped off their shoes at the door.

The room was lain out with a white circular pattern in tile on the ground. There was no electricity — just candles that gave off a pungent woody smell so thick that she grew queasy breathing it in.

At the center of the circle lay a square copper basin about a meter wide on each side. Around it, Dēnasa had positioned offering bowls and trays. The installed statues of the Triad at the back of the temple had the same patterns across their skin as the jar, not stopping near their sensory organs — the web-like pattern covered them completely.

Dēnasa led Tilsa to a position towards the left and just beyond the doors, and le positioned Tilōno towards the right. One of the carved balls found its way into her hands, and she didn't remember Dēnasa putting it there. Her thoughts were interrupted by the thud of the door as le shut them all in.

She could hardly see in the flickering candlelight. The ceiling above them could have been shrouded in shadow or the nothingness of space for all she knew.

Dēnasa approached the statues at the front of the ritual space. Le incanted in a language that sounded almost like Classical Atarahi, but with a halting quality to its vowels that wasn't quite right. The pronouns and affixes were nearly the same. She just couldn't grab the content of the words themselves beyond a vague familiarity.

Dēnasa struck a gong at the foot of the statues three times. The air took on a chill. Until now, the ćas in the herbal mixture had made her feel roomy and safe. There wasn't enough ćas in the world to make a cold like this feel like anything other than something from which she should run.

"Offer the balls," Dēnasa whispered. "Tell them what you want."

Dēnasa placed three of the balls down in front of the Gods and said, "For the performance of the ritual to awaken texts that have been lost, misplaced, or destroyed, to awaken the words bound within character-shapes."

Tilsa walked forward, prostrated before each of the statues, and added ler ball to the pile. "For the resurrection of a text that will show us a good example of what has been lost from the *Records from the Oracle at Tuðá*, along with providing the most time-sensitive oracular advice among what has gone missing." The binding over ler mouth muffled the words, but they still carried.

Tilōno approached the shrine. She prostrated and nearly caught the hem of her coat on something sharp in the semidarkness as she came up. A chill ran down her spine as she added the ball. "I want to have the missing pages, to reunite them with the texts, because ō Ćedīsam should not be deprived of oracles, and your temple-library has been profaned if such things are allowed to happen."

Tilsa breathed in sharply when Tilōno turned around. Ler face indicated that le was angry, but Tilōno was beyond caring. Tilsa may have paid for this. Tilsa may have come from a librarian family, with connections and an understanding of the risks beyond anything that Tilōno could fathom. Le might be descended from Adīsa, *belonging to Sa*. Le might have borne the name *Tilsa, Sa-like*, but le was nothing like the deity who presided over the House of Books, the one who guarded the Libraries of Heaven, Sa whose chariot was drawn by hāyiko.

She took her position again.

Dēnasa stood before the table. Le smashed ler fist down into the center of the balls.

They shattered.

Wood, beautiful and painted, just gone — and what lay in their wake glinted like stardust or pulverized computing equipment, choking the shrine in defiance of gravity.

The candles went out.

It was so cold that her teeth chattered, so cold that breath would not suck itself into her lungs. She fought for air. The room took on on a frosty sheen, light coming from everywhere and nowhere, scattered by the particulates all around them. Her breath came out like frost and in like tiny daggers.

Dēnasa's mouth moved. Le was chanting. It was impossible to hear lim because there was no air, and yet there was, just as there was no more light and yet was. Dēnasa knelt in front of the copper basin with the jar. A sheet of paper floated around lim like a halo. There were beings somewhere, moving so slowly in the darkness that they may have been figments of Tilōno's imagination.

The liquid should have frozen instantaneously on hitting the copper. It was cold enough that Tilōno had already lost sensation in her fingers. Something that looked like blood trickled from Dēnasa's nose.

The ink spilled into the copper and began to float. It filled the room in tiny droplets like shards, and the paper floated out into the center of the ritual space just above them. The ink made its way to that paper, spiraling like dancers around divine images in ritual, combining into words and coming apart again as the ink moved. Gradually, the text on the page emerged, both front and back, blossoming like fleeting flowers. A paragraph coalesced here, a character there.

When it stopped, the paper began to fall downward, arcing back and forth. It would have drowned itself in the ink had Tilsa not lunged out to catch it. Ler chin was bloody. Tilōno suddenly felt the wetness at her own lips, its metallic taste.

Dēnasa met Tilōno's eyes, but it was not Dēnasa in them. What occupied ler eyes were the wild hāyiko and the tame āyiki who followed Tilōno around her home, the branches that produced traditional paper and the factories that created nābimī. The one in Dēnasa smiled. When le breathed out, blood bubbled on Dēnasa's lips.

"The librarian is like a diver, whose time is spent plunging down beneath the pressure of all of the texts that have come before lim. What cannot be destroyed can only sink beyond all easy sighting, on the ocean floor where to be forgotten is akin to having been destroyed. There, the many-limbed and many-tentacled make their beds, scavenging for food that they will then take above. You have always had what you needed to bring back the things that are missing. Always."

Tilōno broke eye contact. She blinked. Dēnasa inhaled sharply, like someone who had not breathed in a long time. The air flooded back into the room, and along with it the candlelight reawakened. The air made a *pop* as it came back.

The offering balls were gone. The copper panel in the center of the room was coated with a small layer of ink, most still in the vessel at Dēnasa's side.

Tilsa clutched the paper.

Tilōno started shaking. The room was still cold, but it was Maqáng's autumnal cold, not the sublime, terrifying other whom she'd seen in the dark chambers of Dēnasa's eyes.

*

Outside of the brick building, Dēnasa collapsed. Tilsa rushed forward and pulled lim up to ler feet. The inked paper pressed against their bodies. Tilōno grabbed it out of the crook of Tilsa's elbow. Blood ran down Dēnasa's chin from ler mouth and nose, and the sides of ler head were wet and dark with it, too.

The esotericist was still conscious. In the dim light, ler skin had a pallid sheen that made the tattoos even more prominent on ler face. She put the paper in a pocket and helped prop Dēnasa up.

They lay Dēnasa inside the other building in a small bed. Tilsa went to a small box and pulled out a diagnostic robot. Le handed it to Tilōno, who turned it on and set it to work on Dēnasa. She didn't ask how Tilsa knew it was there. From her parents, she knew that exes could be complicated, moving in and out of lives like unraveling threads.

"You should have said that you'd already done cold work in the message you sent me, not just *okay, great*, Dēn." Tilsa gritted ler teeth shut and shook ler head. "We could have come at some other time. It's not like you're desperate for money like a few years ago when this started. And you're not—"

"Young anymore?" Dēnasa laughed, and it turned into a cough.

The robot let itself beneath ler robes and moved under the fabric. Its movements reminded Tilōno of small monsters in horror movies. She almost couldn't keep herself still. Her body still felt shaky, and it hurt to breathe.

Tilōno sat down on her knees and pressed her hands beneath her folded legs. She rocked slightly, steadying herself in that rhythm.

"What I mean is that doing things like that could get you killed. You're not an oracle. Each of them has an entire team of physicians. You see *exactly one* physician whom you don't even like." Tilsa locked eyes with Tilōno. She looked away, but the sselē started talking anyway. "And you. That question that you asked. Write down the answer. You shouldn't have asked something that complicated without fucking warning lim, especially once we'd had the attention of a God. What the fuck is wrong with you? Dēnasa could be really hurt."

"I have paper in the writing desk," Dēnasa murmured.

Tilōno nodded. She stood up and retrieved a sheet of paper and a fountain pen. Dēnasa's pens all used maroon or amber ink, Sasnē's sacred colors. She chose an amber one and wrote, *Librarians like divers who plunge down. Texts have pressure because there are other people. Some things aren't destroyed, but there's detritus on the ocean floor. They can be scavenged. I have what I need to grab them.* It wasn't nearly as poetic as the original.

The robotic first aid responder chirruped and climbed out of Dēnasa's robes near ler feet. It made its way to a tethered tablet across the room and connected itself. Tilōno picked up both of them and read the display.

"The robot will monitor lim every half-hour. There's some minor bleeding." She slid her finger up to scroll. "It recommends seeking medical attention. Internal bleeding complication risk."

Tilsa's lips curled up in disdain. "Here we go," le whispered as le breathed out.

"I'm not seeing a doctor," Dēnasa said.

"You're coughing up blood from your lungs." Tilsa sighed. "Do you really want to die like this? Calling Gods into yourself in the middle of the woods? Dying of exposure?"

"*A* deity. Sa, probably."

"Fine. Sa." Tilsa rose to ler feet. "Tilōno, put down the medical device."

Tilōno's eyes widened. "We're seriously leaving lim here?"

Tilsa looked down at Dēnasa. The esotericist's breathing had become regular again, but that didn't mean anything. Tilōno trusted the robot more than appearances. Tilsa's gaze moved down Dēnasa's torso and rested on ler heaving chest. While Tilsa's facial expression was neutral, teary eyes betraying at least a hint of worried anger. Le didn't cry, though. It was probably something about falling out of love that held lim back from doing more.

She hoped that she'd never look this way at Sīyas. There was too much anger in ler eyes. She wondered if all love turned to poison.

Dēnasa sighed. "Put down the robot and my tablet. Close to me, if it's all the same to you."

She approached the bed and placed them within ler reach. "You're not internally bleeding anywhere very serious, right?"

"You skimmed my medical readout, so you tell me."

Tilōno looked down at the tablet again. She barely took the words in. She wasn't a medical professional or health sciences librarian. Tilsa stood behind her like a raging volcano, perhaps ready to burst, and that didn't help. She could see the flex and clench of ler fist. "No. Or maybe."

"If you'd held me in there longer than that, it would probably be different," Dēnasa said gently. "Whatever Sa told you, pay attention to it. The God doesn't like it when ler advice goes unused."

She nodded. "Okay."

Dēnasa nodded. "You'll be back, Ussēta Tilōno."

"You're not an oracle and you don't know that. Let's go, Tilōno." Tilsa stomped one foot on the ground.

Tilōno's heart thudded hard in her chest. "Goodbye, Ussēta Nivssēkabī Dēnasa."

Tilsa didn't say goodbye. It seemed marvelous that le hadn't yelled at Dēnasa inside or at *her* on the way out. There was a teary-eyed tantrum blazing just beneath the surface, though, fueled by sleeplessness and stress.

They were silent for a long time as they walked. The horizon's edge grew pale. They wouldn't have much time to prepare for work.

A small pack of hāyiko followed them to the forest's edge, but stayed back. Most humans had livestock prods with them when they went into wild spaces, and the hāyiko had learned not to bother them. Tilōno thought of her warm bed and Kalðī, who often snuggled up beside her. She didn't want to go to work.

It was only once they returned to the sidewalk that Tilsa said, "You need to be very exact about what you say to a God. They're expansive beings, and if you bring certain requests into a ritual space, you can't know what will happen. You don't want Gods to ride someone like an oracle when le doesn't have training or a medical team present."

"It's happened before, though?"

"Twice, once with me, once with someone else. That someone else nearly got lim killed." Tilsa let in a breath, held it, and sighed it out. "Nobody knows what a God is, but what they are is infinitely good and expansive and — everything — and that can spell disaster for ordinary people. Imagine trying to fit that all in a human body. It burns up. I don't understand it at all, but it is that way, or so it seems."

Tilōno held that paradox in her head. A God was like a hurricane, she posited, or a supernova. Both were necessary and good. She wasn't a philosopher or theologian, and even after that experience, she didn't want to know what they would say about Gods and cold. She never wanted to be in a space like that again, and yet she craved to be in a space like that again. She wanted her fingertips to hug the prayer beads while she intoned names. She wanted the names to be filled with that. In retrospect, the cold was a lot like bliss. "I'm sorry."

"Are you? You got the information you wanted."

"I didn't know that it would hurt lim. I wanted it, but not at that cost." The guilt landed in her stomach hard. She had to navigate through what Sa had said. "But we have a page."

Tilsa nodded. "Give it to me."

She reached into her coat pocket and took it out. The print was an exact duplicate of the *Records from the Oracle at Tuðá*'s formatting and font, which was uncanny. Both the front and back described ō Ćedīsam.

They stopped in the middle of the street beneath a winternut tree, whose seed pods had already begun to swell. Tilsa pulled a flashlight out of ler pocket and read the page silently. The only things that moved were ler eyebrows. They showed surprise once, maybe twice. Le murmured *oh shit* only once.

"What do you think?" she asked.

"I think that someone is stealing oracular texts related to preparations for the upcoming elections," Tilsa said, "because all of this is a set of admonitions and advice to ō Ćedīsam on proper conduct during their lead-up. There's a negotiation of some kind, a heart-yielding moment. Someone will have a strong emotion, and that will lead to a breakdown somewhere. It will be a disaster for ō Ćedīsam."

"How old is the oracle?"

Tilsa handed her the page. The date was up at the top. It had been given two years earlier, well into the planning cycle for an electoral campaign for high office. It described ritual impurity and improper conduct too much to merely describe election fallout. Something had happened on a more human level, and their success was at risk from ordinary ritual impurities and feuds festering. The ō Ćedīsam family needed to redress someone's grievances. Something endangered a *Zaćibamlē*, whatever that was — a conscious effort to remain hidden and quiet, but the word had a programmatic connotation. Tilōno's gaze rested uneasily on that word. It sounded familiar. Tekīya had used that word.

This was just enough to make her want to know what this family did in politics, whose political campaigns they backed, and what they ran for. The Demzang nobility occupied a tenuous space between the old, post-Empire ways and the new popular rule. Sīyas might know something from the inside, but she might not tell Tilōno.

"Do you know anything about the family's politics?"

"They own a fair amount of property," Tilsa said, "and they have significant influence. One of their senior members, Bēhel, is the most likely candidate for Chancellorship. They don't always see the perspective of the people."

"In what ways?"

"They have some strange relationships with Ural. There's a younger member who married an Urang diplomat from their nobility. It's widely believed to have been a bad move, perhaps because there was active courtship from a non-noble merchant family. It was seen as hostile to the post-war environment," Tilsa said, "because they marry for—"

"Life, unless something bad happens. I know that." Tilōno sighed. "I know an ō Ćedīsam. That's not why I'm stressed about this. Um, Sīyas, a young composer. She's half Urang. She did ask if I knew anything about the family oracles. I didn't know how much to tell her. But I don't see why an oracle would be talking about marital disasters. It's a non-issue from what I've seen."

"Maybe in Owá. This is the capital." Tilsa nodded. "Sīyas must be their child. There's stuff about — her? — in the tabloids."

"Her, yeah," Tilōno muttered. She pulled out the piece of paper with Sa's advice on it and read over the writing, which she had done in women's script. The jarring lines looked like claw-scratches from how swiftly she had jotted it all down. *Diving into data.* She smiled. The lines connected suddenly or she was so tired that anything seemed like a solution. "This is funny, you know. I never would have thought of it."

Tilsa frowned. "What?"

"We dive when we connect live to the data stream. We hold our consciousness together while we answer questions that the AI routines can't." She folded the paper into quarters and placed it back in her coat pocket. "There's the data we seek, and then there's the data that is found along the way and kept for five years for the large audit before being discarded. The environmental stuff. Making sure the robots touch the right pages, that sort of thing. Like with what you're doing with the AI — it was answering questions it shouldn't have."

"What are you getting at?"

"What if the texts were not ultimately stolen from the House of Books? What if they were just razored out and hidden in other ones? Or better yet, what if the AI answered questions and they're in the audit trail somewhere?" The more she said, the more it sounded right. "Hiding pages in the compact shelving is disruptive because the pages are not where they should be. Cleaning bots don't check inside books, and robots' programs don't flag tip-ins. And you said the AI has been doing things it shouldn't. The bots are moving through the shelves constantly. People at high levels of clearance love consulting remotely."

She thought through it. She didn't know how long a dive would take, especially since the ad hoc use terminals for librarians were less up-to-date than the ones used for hours at a time during reference shifts. She could last four hours in a jittery terminal on a full night's sleep. That wasn't today. She was still wired, but eventually, she'd fatigue. If she went in now, she could perhaps last two before the safety jettisoned her out of the dive.

Tilsa went still. Le looked in the direction of the tracks and started walking, gaze lowered, hands fighting into ler pockets. One of the cold-weather piercings in ler left ear looked like an esoteric offering balls in miniature. She would ask so may questions about what those offering balls meant if she had the time. They were nothing like any votive she had ever seen.

She hurried to catch up to Tilsa.

"Ural does not interlibrary loan its oracular texts," Tilsa said softly. "Do you know anyone from Đeza? They've done it in the past on rare occasions. It would be easier if we could just ask someone to go to the archives there. All I have to do is mention the Zaćibamlē, and I think we're in."

Đeza was Demza's other neighbor, and they'd split apart long before the war, with separate Chancellors reporting to the Empire well before space travel stopped. She could see the shape of the marker for Đeza's capital city, but couldn't recall its name. Vesh, perhaps, unless that was just its southernmost port.

"You know what that means?"

"It's the planetary security initiative that keeps us planetlocked. It's why we don't have ambient networks or radio." Tilsa looked suddenly uncomfortable. "You'll learn more about it. You have green clearance now. It's not something Atara wants private citizens to care about. Anything endangering the Zaćibamlē is very dire."

"What's your plan?" Tilōno asked.

"We're addressing this today. I hate it when things drag out. I'll message your morning supervisor and ask if you can be relieved for specialized task work. You'll do the deep dive."

"Why not you?"

"I hate data-diving." Tilsa paused. "I used to like it a lot more before Dēnasa and I fell out. The deep spaces remind me of lim."

Tilōno had nothing to say to that. She focused on the thoughts bouncing around her head in chaos. It was useless to tie them together while so tired. There were two of them, though. Two people should be able to work together. "What will you do while I'm under?"

"Someone stole those oracular texts. We don't know if it was a library user or a staff member." Tilsa breathed in through ler teeth. "My guess is staff, and we have so many in the library that it would be hard to limit it to anyone specific. Twenty or so people. Or maybe up to fifty. It's hard to say."

"ID swipe records?"

"No." Tilsa looked ahead towards the rail request pole. They were too far away to make out the arrival times on the readout. "There's a complication. People are nice. They hold doors for people they recognize even when they shouldn't."

"I guess so."

Tilsa clicked ler tongue. "I'm going to interlibrary loan everything from Ðeza immediately. If a library staff member stole them, le might intercept what we put in the system. I'm hoping le does something careless in a panic. It will trigger the audit system, which I can see. I have violet clearance. The only ones above me are the Planetary Coordination Authority, haribātna, and qēssen."

A train started to move towards the station in the distance. Tilsa broke into a run, and Tilōno ran behind lim. She was out of breath by the time they reached the request pole, just in time to signal it to stop.

She sat down beside Tilsa towards the back of the car. The crowd this early looked mostly like professionals, with some temple dancers, religious officiants, and schoolchildren. A few of the professionals wore scholars' robes. It probably wasn't safe to talk.

ॐ

Tilōno checked her messages as soon as she arrived home — three from Sīyas and two from Tekīya. One of Tekīya's contained two simple spreadsheets, and the other was a long-winded ramble that roved among a discussion of friendship boundaries, concern for the āyiki, and some political thing happening in Owá that Tilōno would need to research before getting too angry about. She highlighted the passages that she needed to respond to and saved the annotations in the Registry in private mode so he wouldn't see them.

Tilōno showered. She skimmed the spreadsheets while getting ready. Ō Ćedīsam spent money continuously. Ō Đōtam, a family that often appeared after them and which also had missing pages, had skipped two half-years over the past ten years. Tilōno would need to check those against the evidence. Most important families supported at least three oracles. Ō Ćedīsam supported five. Tilōno fastened her scholar's robes final buttons and transferred the knife from the night's clothes into her pocket.

Two drunken messages from Sīyas rambled on, location-stamped from a holographic garden. Tilōno hadn't even realized that it was possible to cable in when visiting places like that — all of the emphasis was on the shows and the dissociative neural arrays that people wore, holdovers from the Sāqab Empire's glory days. It wasn't out of the question that there'd be cable hookups in the booths. She had only ever been to one twice.

The third message said, *Could you come over to dinner with my family tomorrow night? I've been invited to the primary meal, and I'm allowed to bring a guest.*

Tomorrow. That would have been *today* based on the

question's timestamp.

Tilōno's family in Demza was too small for primary meals, notwithstanding that Midwayers didn't segregate members of the family according to status. There were no primary and secondary meals. She and Sīyas were dating now, so it made sense that she go. *Yes. What time? Do I need to dress for anything specific? Is it a talking ritual or a secular dinner?*

Kalðī jumped on the bed as she pressed enter on the message. She needed to meet Tilsa at the train and commute into work. Sīyas responded immediately. *In the second hour of night. You can wear scholar's robes if necessary, but it's not a ritual.*

While transferring the message's details into her calendar, she mentally inventoried her closet. She owned one outfit formal enough for visiting the nobility, a long-sleeved shirt made of moodcloth with a pair of black pants that gathered at the ankles, both stitched in the Midway geometric style, but heavy enough for Maqáng autumn. It might be too Midway for the Demzang nobility.

Okay, I'll be there. By that night, she might even have something to say about the oracle.

Tilōno took some caffeine pills from the dispensary downstairs and put them in the pocket of her scholar's robes. She made her oblations in the prayer room. A few other young scholars prayed in front of the Triad, too. One was petitioning for a manuscript blessing. She nearly fell asleep to the *tick, tick, tick* of the beads along the metal wire as she moved through the epithets of the Gods.

She found Tilsa sitting on a bench just inside of the weather overhang by the train tracks, tethered in and responding to messages in the Registry. The sselē looked up at her, but didn't smile.

"Are you ready to dive?" le asked. "I got permission."

"Are you ready to make the interlibrary loan request?" she responded.

Tilsa smirked. "I did that already."

"Sīyas ō Ćedīsam, the young woman I met on the train, invited me over for dinner. She asked me to go steady," Tilōno said casually. Her heart raced. "Is this a conflict of interest? It's okay, right?"

"It's fine, but you should be careful." Tilsa rolled ler eyes. "You're on a romantic *date* with her family."

"Yes."

"She's in the nobility." Tilsa chuckled. "She reached out because her elders asked. They know that she's courting you."

Tilōno's brow furrowed. Her thoughts twisted her in a thousand directions at once, and for a moment, all she could manage was a glare. She collected herself. "We've known each other for barely a heartbeat. That's *witless*." It had been on the forefront of her mind. No messing around with matchmakers' dances and the genetic compatibility AI. Just Sīyas. She didn't know which was harder to commit to.

"I'm Maqáng. I know these things." Tilsa rose to ler feet and jutted ler chin towards the crowd collecting at the platform. "We should make this train."

As the train pulled in, Tilōno counted her breaths and focused on the sensation of her feet against the platform. It was important to be centered before diving into data, to fashion her selfhood into an unbreakable net, so she could stand immobile as rock in the torrent. She couldn't rely on caffeine pills for everything. Too much caffeine and the cracking anxiety in her chest would threaten to drown her and activate the machine safety protocols — although, she could dive *without* safety if she had to. Today might be that day.

Tilsa spent the entire ride reading a digital poetry book, lips pressed together tightly. The interlinear notation looked like oratorical annotations, the half-musical style that told a reader what to stress in a performance. It wasn't religious poetry even though it was definitely Classical Atarahi, not Demaí. Religious poetry never used words like *ća* or the pronoun *ramis*. It was raunchy and coarse reading.

She knew so little about the person she'd dragged into the fight for oracles beyond that it was ler duty just as much as hers. It wasn't like dealing with Tekīya, whose temper was consistently bad in a way that Tilōno could manage almost effortlessly after nearly a decade of experience. Tilōno couldn't see Tekīya reading anything vulgar.

They arrived at the library and waited through the opening ritual. Tilōno discreetly swallowed a caffeine tablet just as it finished. She and Tilsa walked in behind the religious officiants. Her heart pounded from anticipation, and not even counting breaths could calm it.

They parted near reference. Tilōno passed by the spot she usually used. She was first in the line for the as-need-be terminals, so she had her pick. The one she chose was an older design that librarians in Owá still used. If she had to turn off the safety, she wanted it to be via a system she knew like a favorite shirt.

She lay back in the case. Before she connected, she took deep belly breaths in through the nose, each held for what felt like an infinity before she exhaled. The implant in the back of her neck itched. She pressed the *go* button and the unit closed her in. Everything around her was a dark cocoon, the hand controls minimal. The system connected itself to her like an ūnor diving from the sky to snare its claws beneath the shore-waves. The physical world dissipated.

It was data, just as before, just as always, but in the on-demand, there were no reference questions waiting to capture her attention and steal it for hours on end. She was a presence within a vibrating mass of information, the robotic assistants on each level of the library waiting to assist with their print collections, the system itself alive and watching her as she watched it. Tilōno had no body here, only a sense of heaviness and breath.

She called up the data stream, the extent limited to the Hall of Oracles. A mess of past reference questions rose up in a cyclone around her. Family concerns. Queries about specific towns or cities. A divination audit for one of the rail lines. There were security level marks beside each one. The indigo and black-level clearance questions were redacted smears. The violet ones were pixelated. The green, visible.

It was so much information. Elsewhere, or inside of herself, her heart hammered. The caffeine was kicking in. A notification popped up warning her of her mental state. It was too early to turn off the safety.

She pushed deeper. Data flowed through her like tiny razors made of paper. Below that lay the guts of the robotic systems and the press of the AI systems, hungry for reference questions within the Hall.

Deeper still, she decided, in the mess of audit controls. A voice whispered, *Warning: You have entered an area where nothing may be deleted.* The notification center activated again. She had to calm down. Her body felt so far away, and it wasn't listening.

Tilōno hovered in a thousand million shards of information, none cataloged. The AI routines flitted like predatory birds in the shadows. She formulated a question in pseudo-AI speak.

She needed images of pages that were wrong. Torn pages. Ear-tips. Inserts that were not already accounted for in object metadata. Stray sheets obscuring text. Just the Hall of Oracles. If she didn't restrict her data to that location, the entire library of damaged and misplaced things would enter her, and she could drown.

The seventeen thousand eighty-three results in queue *hurt*. AI threw pages at her with abandon, and she was sliced by data sheet after data sheet, a torrent of misplaced nābimī and forgotten request reminders and visitors' yellowed, personal tip-in notes. Some things dated to before the ship-grounding, and she fought not to distract herself. The sky didn't matter. The Atarahi in those early-colony notes was different, with a few letters she didn't recognize. AI would give her what she focused on, and she couldn't afford to investigate *that* right now.

Tilōno oriented the results spatially: a queue in the foreground, discards behind. To her left, she kept the pages that she found. The first one that mentioned ō Ćedīsam made her heart sing. It was misshapen, though, the paper folded in half, with no scans of the missing sides. Then she located a second, and then a third. There would be forty-six in total in the mass of ephemera. It was so much to see. She added location codes from the audit to each recovered page and told the bots where to query.

Warning: The Hall of Oracles is experiencing a disturbance and has initiated staff workstation evacuation protocols. AI access will shut down in two minutes. Please save your work.

Tilōno stopped the flow of documents. *What kind of disturbance?*

Security AI has reported violent activity. Please save your work. Remember to avoid the Hall of Oracles while human security is called to de-escalate the situation.

Tilsa, she thought to herself. The interlibrary loan request. The seconds ticked down to her lower right. Two minutes wasn't enough time.

She found the robotics in the Hall of Oracles and asked, *Is Tilsa okay?* Tilōno accessed the robots' sensory organs. Humans were writhing in the stacks, screaming and yelling as blows connected with flesh. There was water. A pipe must have burst, or perhaps —

A fire has been reported in the Hall of Oracles. Building evacuation is now mandatory for all staff and visitors. Safety shutdown is recommended for all podded librarians.

Her heart beat so fast. There were more notifications now. Cognitive and emotional overload, bad for staying focused while diving into the depths of data. Ejection recommended.

She became aware of herself in the claustrophobic pod, the connection between herself and the skeletal cables at the base of her neck. *No,* she thought, but in the data stream, it sounded like a scream.

The only thing to do was to plunge in full throttle, processing the results as if taking all of them in through her mouth. Tilōno couldn't even feel her heart anymore. Cold grew all around her.

Ninety seconds remaining. Twenty-three of the forty-six, halfway done. She was a human mind, not an AI, and her power in this situation was not infinite. It was fatiguing to be here.

Sa, God of the libraries and keeper of the house of books for She of Many Texts, please be with me. Sasnē and Sanwū, please do not abandon me now. She needed to move faster.

Tilōno turned off the safety. The notification screen minimized itself.

It was like being in a room where everyone was shouting, in an ink pool drowning, and a child again standing among all of those forlorn archival documents in Tekīya's laboratory. It was the mystery initiation and a crowd of hāyiko preparing to lunge. It was Kalƌī begging for food in the early morning. It was the data cables breaking beneath the waves over and over, the current and seafloor breaking all things apart. The data moved around her, smothering her, drowning her. There was nowhere to go but *down*.

Typography. The pages looked unique. She had to find them — markings that separated pages — years and seasons — missing. She reached out to grab infinity and found only darkness beyond.

Her blood roared in her ears, and the sensors yelled something at her. It wouldn't automatically remove her without the safety. That was it. Eighteen seconds. Forty-one texts.

She centered her consciousness in breath. Eighteen seconds. *Come at me,* she thought, *and show me what lies in wait from the oracle at Tuðá.*

Tilōno reached the bottom. It felt like solid ground. The world transformed into a bare-bones VR experience. Texts swirled around her like birds taking wing. It was a plain so dark that she might as well have been standing in the center of an inkwell or the scavenge graveyards in Owá that had once held advanced wireless technology, now only spare parts. Information made piles as high as mountains.

And it was cold. So cold that the pages had frost on them, so cold that Tilōno's breath came cold in front of her. Her lungs ached with the memory of that night with Dēnasa.

This is digital, she thought. Nine seconds. Nothing made a sound. *I'm in a simulation. This isn't real.*

But it wasn't what users could see. It wasn't the abstract data stream she knew as a librarian. She could feel herself again, and she felt like flesh and blood, not consciousness.

Tilōno twisted and turned in a circle to take all of the texts in. She grabbed one out of the air. Two. Her numb hands made it hard to feel the weight of the nābimī in her hands. The third hovered almost out of reach, and digital gravity held her down. She hunted through the shuddering mass of paper with one hand. Four, hidden behind some pages that had printing damage.

She twisted and turned, and as she walked, the paper followed her. There was no way to go *up*. Nine. Seconds.

She knelt down and stared at the blackness at her feet. The cold was almost heart-shattering, and a part of her wondered if the ink on the pages in her digital hands would lift and spill around her. She thought of Dēnasa with the God inside of lim, that moment when something had stared at her from beyond the abyss.

The paper collapsed in heaps. Still nine seconds. Still the illusion of digitally breathing. Still the cold all around her. She saw movement and looked up.

Someone else was here, ler bare feet making ink footprints as le walked upon the detritus. Le had black hair that fell in locked coils. Le wore a white shroud already stained with ink exuded by each of ler body's pores, and despite the blackness of the ink that covered lim, le glowed with fresh, warm light. This light illuminated the massive piles of images and digital data all around them. The only color came from ler maroon eyes. Nine seconds.

She felt so awake, so alive.

The cold made the air pulsate.

The being held out a single page.

Tilōno closed the distance between them. She grabbed the paper between her thumb and index finger. No sound came from her mouth. She used the digital system instead. *May I have this?*

The being released it. The paper was even colder than the air around it. Tilōno looked down. Nine seconds.

You're not an AI, are you? You're Sa.

The eyes blinked. Le had six of them suddenly, like a hāyiko.

When the God spoke, it was with the sound of quaking pages and of humming servers. It was the entire digital architecture come alive, the perfume of old books, and the strength of nābimī paper. Tilōno saw the deep floors of the digital infrastructure in the darkness and felt the presences of the librarians who had left traces of themselves in the system for generations. She sensed the clockwork-like regularity of the AI, its various personalities answering questions from everyone in Demza with alacrity and speed. Her veins were the data connections to the scientific labs and engineering firms, the musicians and composers, even her family's home in Owá.

The physicality of the library weighed Tilōno down. She could not move her legs. Sa was a fishing net, and she was caught in lim. There was no difference between the digital and analog spaces. Oracles could see both. Officiants could see both. What was Tilōno now that she had met a God's eyes, diving into the House of Books? What would she do for *lim*?

The God's mouth closed.

Nine seconds.

The data moved beneath her and around her. She held the sheet. The other missing ones floated around her like a halo, all forty-five of them. The final page. Forty-six. Everything.

Thank you, Tilōno thought.

Sa dissipated into ink. The cold evaporated. Her heart thudded in her throat. The virtual world began to crumble, and then it was gone. There was no VR landscape in the librarians' interface, just the unadulterated stream of data. Eight seconds. Eight.

She thought, *Print queue with metadata to personal account and paper backup.* The first time, it added the page images to the queue — each of them ineffective on their own, as the nābimī was folded and creased, and the robots had only seen part of most sheets. She canceled the job — that was not the correct request. It was better to have a list of places the papers could be found in the volumes, so she sent that to the printer instead. Thinking in the onslaught of the entire virtual library matrix made her feel as if she couldn't catch her breath. She reactivated the safety.

Bio signs flagged for injury. Pulse very slow, breathing regular. Adrenaline still high, though. Elevated caffeine levels. Her breath felt wet, ragged. Full. She coughed.

Cutting connection to the Hall of Oracles.

When it split her off, she slammed back into full consciousness in the pod. It knocked the wind out of her. She fought to breathe. The regulatory lights blinked softly all around her in the cocoon, safe and familiar. Slowly, she brought her fingers to her lips. They were wet and warm. Blood.

THIS IS THE LIBRARY FIRE ALERT SYSTEM. THIS IS NOT A DRILL. PLEASE PROCEED TO THE NEAREST EXIT. The emergency evacuation light strobed through the cracks in the pod.

It had been far longer than nine seconds in the company of that God.

Tilōno disengaged from the pod. She untethered her tablet. The room was a mass of library staff pouring towards the exit, practically stampeding. Her legs failed her when she tried to stand up. The room pitched sideways, and everything hurt. She grabbed a tissue from the dispenser beside the pod and wiped her mouth clean of red.

When she found her footing, she set off away from the exit. If Tilsa was there, le needed help.

The door between the reference room and the Hall of Oracles wouldn't open. There had to be a manual override for the emergency, in the very least because if a power outage happened while in lockdown, there might be a catastrophic failure. Lights flashed red and white all around the door. There was a key override, but she didn't have a key.

There wouldn't be another way to the Hall of Oracles from the staff side, just the public. To go around, she'd have to ascend the stairs and use a secondary hallway. The doors there might be locked, too. She remembered the knife in her pocket and pulled it out. It clattered to the ground. Tilōno picked it up. She removed the safety guard and tried to pry the door open. It didn't work.

Tilōno dropped the knife and ran for the staircase.

She took the steps two at a time, clinging to the rail because everything in her body hurt. Nobody remained in the hall to check for stray librarians. It was just her and the ambient robots.

Sirens still blared. At the end of the hall, she took the stairs back down into the main public reading room.

Tilōno stumbled at the bottom. There were policing Sentinels — she counted five at first glance, but there could have been more. They moved with mesmerizing, lethal grace. Tilōno scrambled backwards up the stairs and crouched down by one of the banisters. PCA officers followed the Sentinels in, all about Tilsa's age, none with any kind of piercing. Their shouting echoed against the ceiling.

One Sentinel broke away from the others and ran towards the staircase. Tilōno stumbled to her feet and put her hands above her head, subconsciously recalling the drills from school. At this distance, the Sentinel could identify that she was holding a tablet, not a gun, but it was still terrifying.

Gunshots came from inside the Hall of Oracles. The screams and shouts echoed on the main floor's ceiling. The room suddenly smelled acrid, burnt.

Her arms were tired. The Sentinel at the bottom of the stairs paced, guns locked to her movements. She closed her eyes and tried to picture that room with Sa again. It calmed her down.

Someone grabbed her from behind. She nearly dropped the tablet. The Sentinel retracted its guns.

A haribān pulled her up the stairs and back into the hallway. The haribān wrenched the tablet out of Tilōno's hand, red eyes wide with concern. It was a woman whom Tilōno had never seen before.

"They told me that there was a fight," the haribān said. "Tilōno, are you okay?"

"I wasn't there," she murmured. The Sentinel outside made metal-on-stone noises as it climbed the stairs up towards the second level. "Tilsa, Hāyin, Hūtong — they must all be there. How do you know who I am?"

The haribān sighed. "I have known you since you were nine, Ussēta Tilōno." The edge in her voice was palpable.

Haribātna. Body-switching. "Tekīya," she murmured. "It's you."

The smile on the woman's dark brown face broke into a grin. She, or he-in-she, pulled Tilōno close. It was at once comfortable and familiar and alien. The tablet in the haribān's hand pressed into her back.

The Sentinel reached the top of the stairs. Tekīya-in-she barely acknowledged it, but Tilōno's tensed.

More gunfire from downstairs.

"I thought you didn't switch bodies for your friends because we might take advantage of your connections," Tilōno murmured. Her eyes stung, and the world blurred together. She might cry. "What is this, then?"

Tekīya kissed her forehead and drew back. The Sentinel remained still. "The lockdown at the Maqá National Library was mentioned in the collective. I care about you, Tilōno."

She wiped tears away from her eyes. "I have the data. Which books." She nodded her chin at the tablet in Tekīya's right hand. "So as long as we have that, it's fine."

Tekīya sighed. "Relax, then? You're so wired all the time." Tekīya-in-she pressed the tablet into the pocket of Tilōno's robes.

She wouldn't have dared pull it back out in front of a Sentinel.

She'd read the safety announcements that every child was drilled with from a young age. Tekīya and the haribānōqi woman he inhabited seemed comfortable in front of it, but she could never be.

The doors slammed open again. There were more sirens. Tilōno remained still and looked at the Sentinel. "Is my boss all right?"

It said nothing.

A boom made the floor shudder. Screams this time, definitely not shouts.

Tilōno had nothing to do but wait. In her head, negative self-talk shouted horrible things. She had drawn Tilsa into this. It hadn't been resolved quietly like le wanted. Now, everyone would know what had happened here. Everyone would know that someone had stolen nābimī.

CHAPTER SIX

When the skirmish stopped, Tekīya and the Sentinel brought Tilōno downstairs. Medics carried someone out in a body bag. She grabbed Tekīya-in-she's hand — the bag was perhaps Tilsa's size, perhaps not. The morning light coming through the windows had a surreal edge to it, and everything it hit had a sense of wrongness. She felt like she needed to scrub her skin clean. Part of her wanted to run over to the small Triad and Reed shrines and cover them. With Sentinels here, she could not.

A doctor set up a portable treatment area on one of the reading room tables. Le wasn't Sāqab. While le wore the gender-neutral clothing and hairstyles open to non-initiates, there was something off — but everyone in the Planetary Coordination Authority had that strange genericness about them. Le activated an android once the table was set up, and it waited patiently while le prepared.

Tilsa came out on a stretcher carried by two medics. They

brought lim directly to the table and the waiting doctor. There was blood everywhere, and they set to work on Tilsa's arm and torso by cutting loose ler ruined garments. Tilsa, still conscious, was writhing, and the android had to hold lim down while it administered a topical analgesic.

Tilōno grimaced and held Tekīya-in-she's hand tighter. Her mind raced. Tilsa was hurt, and le needed someone. It was too chaotic for anyone to have called ler family. Le had a child at home.

"You should go to your boss," Tekīya said, almost as if he could hear her thoughts.

She let go of his host's hand and walked towards the table. The android and doctor barely glanced up at her. The doctor was a haribān — unsurprising considering the number of haribānōqi doctors in the First Cities. It was an oversampling she'd first noticed at about eleven after realizing that most of Tekīya's housemates in Owá practiced medicine like her parents, and Tekīya had told young Tilōno that most haribātna in medical professions had gone to school for it after joining the collective, not before. Something about that collective made all of them do it. Their primary leader on the distant planet Ameisa, Arieḥ, took particular interest in medicine.

Tilsa looked up at Tilōno. Ler chest and right sleeve were bare, android already layering bio-stitches into deep cuts on ler arm while it scanned an incision on ler torso. Tilōno suspected that the weapon had been a book scalpel.

She reached for Tilsa's good hand and squeezed it. Tilsa squeezed back with a viselike grip.

"This is what you were thinking when you said you'd draw lim out to do something stupid?" Tilōno asked softly.

The doctor looked up at Tilōno, then beyond her. Tekīya was now at her side. The two haribātna nodded at each other. Tilōno knew enough to understand that there was a telepathic conversation — and if not that, some spill of information from one to the other.

She turned to Tekīya. "Do you know what happened?"

Tilsa groaned and clenched ler teeth together. "I can answer. I'm not *that* out of it. Someone has been monitoring interlibrary loan requests. I set the delivery location to the Hall of Oracles, which puts something in the queue, as we had guessed," le said. The android slapped a pain modulator onto the back of ler neck, and le hissed through clenched teeth. "Hāyin was involved. I never imagined she would be. Hūtong, maybe, but not Hāyin."

A weight fell into Tilōno's gut. "Was Hūtong there?"

"Yes. He's the one who stopped Hāyin from cutting my throat. She stabbed him four times. He was already unconscious by the time I arrived at the Hall. They're probably stabilizing him in there to bring to the hospital. And then her homemade diamond blender exploded." Tilsa shut ler eyes. "This fucking hurts."

Tilōno thought back to the two-minute countdown timer. The digital Hall of Oracles had shut down with just enough time for a librarian to finish ler work, but it had felt like hours in that data-rich landscape. "So was it just Hāyin?"

"She's dead." Tilsa shook ler head. "I imagine the Planetary Coordination Authority will get involved, comb through her digital and textual evidence, make some kind of judgment. We'll all be interrogated."

Tekīya said in a hushed voice, "She was being paid by someone. There are credits in her account. Way too many for someone who does paper sculpture as a hobby and who sells from a digital portfolio. Those would just net the standard hobbyist artisan rates."

Tilōno stared at him. "You're volunteering that?"

"It's a criminal case, so you shouldn't spread that beyond all of us, but there will be a lot of interviews with police and peacekeeping forces." Tekīya glanced towards the Sentinels as if seeing them for the first time. Tilōno studied his unfamiliar face. She didn't even know the name of the body he used, just that she was a scholar, not a medical professional.

Tekīya asked, "Have you ever had a Sentinel guard, Ussēta Director?"

Tilsa tried to shake ler head. It did something to the pain modulator, and le drew in a sharp breath instead. It took nearly a minute for lim to speak. "Is this going to potentially hurt my family?"

"Ideally not, but possibly," Tekīya said. "I'm not involved in any security conversations. I'm just listening to them."

"We have young children in the household."

"Most families have young children," Tekīya said. It was strange to hear his cadence in a woman's mouth. It didn't sound as rude as it did when Tekīya spoke in his own body, but then again, she always assumed that women were well-meaning. She probably stereotyped based on appearances more often than she should.

Tilsa studied Tilōno. "When you said you knew people in the haribātna—"

"I've been cleaning his scientific archives since I was nine. Two hundred years of a hāyiko breeding program, with the goal of a domesticated animal that consistently scores above 95% on the temperament test," Tilōno said. "He's a biologist."

Tekīya-in-she shook his head. "Technically a xenobiologist, but the distinction is moot. Tekahiya ohe Muhubī, but I use Tekīya ō Mūssī. It sounds more Atarahi, doesn't it?"

Tilsa nodded. "The one she talks about."

The android took over from the doctor on patching Tilsa up. Its hands had so many fingers that Tilōno's eyes could barely focus on its fast-paced work.

The doctor grabbed Tekīya's host by the arm to take him aside. The two of them stood staring at each other without speaking.

Tilōno sat down on a chair next to Tilsa. "It's not worth being bitter about not hearing them."

"I know that." Tilsa rolled ler eyes.

"I'm sorry I wasn't there, that I was in the data." She looked down at her hands. *But the God told me to dive into the depths.*

Tilsa smirked. "It was better that you weren't there. You're eighteen, and it would have been hard to deal with all of that and protect you at the same time." Le cleared ler throat. "Which would have been my duty as your supervisor and mentor."

"This got messed up, just as you said. Things with the nobility. Do you remember?"

The smirk turned into a shallow laugh. "Yes, I did say that."

"And you still helped."

Tilsa sighed. "I did. The night I saw you making offerings, I'd spoken to my great-grandmother about this. It was out of sight of everyone else in the family, in the greenhouse at the back of our house. She enjoys sitting there to listen to the sounds of nature. She told me that my duty to you as a teacher was important, and that as much as I dreaded supervising an apprentice, if I don't get this right, I'm doing a disservice to the profession and to the Gods. It didn't sit well with me, that conversation."

"Why?"

"I love the sights and the sounds of ordinary moments in the Hall of Oracles. They feel sacred. Gods know it took time for that collection to grow on me." Ler words were slightly slurred together, but still coherent. "That, to me, is as valuable as any click of the beads in my hands, as precious as any incense. It's up to Sa to decide if that is enough. People told me to be ready for administration, coming from my family, but I wasn't."

"I was raised to fix problems when I found them."

"I know now." Tilsa slowly turned ler head and looked at the stitches. "Who knows how long the theft would have gone on without you here. It would have been a big scandal, and someone would have been punished. Probably me."

Tilōno smiled. "But we have the texts. We can call ō Ćedīsam and say that we have found them."

Tilsa opened ler mouth to speak. Instead, le half-coughed, half-laughed. There was enormous bureaucracy, and Tilōno knew that as well as le. She had studied in library school, and that was one of the first things the instructors have said — *house of books, house of paperwork*.

The police and PCA officers opened up the library about an hour later, with the Hall of Oracles still closed off and teeming with PCA officers and their Sentinels. Tilōno went to the printer in the librarians' space to grab the documentation she needed about the pages' locations.

The PCA officer who took Tilōno's statement and led her into the compact shelving was another Midway woman, perhaps five or six years older and definitely the junior member on the team. She wore her uniform awkwardly. Tilōno made a big show out of activating the bots to retrieve the books for them, which they lined up in piles. Some of these volumes were old, from before the spaceflight grounding and nābimī paper.

The fire evidence in the stacks was all from the nābimī paper's section. Only the covers were damaged. Tilōno knew that without even opening one of the volumes. A makeshift bomb in the staff area had caused more damage than the blender.

All of the missing pages were hidden in books, front and back, folded neatly and tucked into random volumes. It was a relief to stand in the Hall of Oracles and know that *she* had helped it become safe. *She* had done the library and Sa a service by rooting out a traitor to information within their midst. The PCA officer tracking her sat down just across from her and went through the volumes with the demeanor of someone who had never bothered with oracles before. She would have looked at them like that, too, months ago.

The other PCA members worked at the crime scene in the catalogers' room, slowly piecing things together. What they didn't know now, they would discover soon.

By late afternoon, she finished writing up notes about the ō Ćedīsam oracles' contents in the reopened reference question request, prompted by the PCA officer to keep the answer in the official information channels. She pressed *send* and leaned back in the chair. Relief flooded through her body as her anxiety wound down. It was done.

&❧

Tekīya arrived in person that evening, just as Tilōno finished applying her piercings and shining her skin in the co-housing bathroom. She wore her formal Midway attire, crisply ironed and starched by one of the building's assistant robots and perfumed with a scent styled after the incense blend used at temples.

Another professional from the house, Yādot, came to the bathroom door and whispered, "You have a haribān after you." She held a stick of meat between her teeth, which she tore away in clumps. Kalðī begged for scraps at her feet.

"I'm not coming after her," Tekīya shouted from the hallway. "Mind yourself, kid!"

Tilōno left the women's bathroom. Tekīya leaned against the hallway wall. He was as sloppily dressed as ever, definitely not material to meet Sīyas' family. It had already been a hard day, and she'd brainstormed a thousand ways to describe what had happened. She was in the news and couldn't hide her involvement. Someone would ask. She had to make her thoughts tidy.

Tekīya looked at her and smiled. "Wow, you look nice."

"I'm going to see Sīyas."

He nodded. "May I walk with you?"

She came to meet him and put her arm over his shoulder, something she'd often done as a girl, but not as a women.

It was hard to think about Tekīya now that she'd seen him funnel into someone else's body like water into a new glass. Part of her wondered how he thought of himself. Ritual was tied to soul, but it was marked in body during that ritual. Tekīya had never done the latter. If he entered a woman's body, was he a jar waiting to be filled? How did the haribātna think of themselves? Was that why Tekīya so rarely wore his Īpahi-style gender piercings? She wouldn't know unless a collective chose to bind her to it.

"I suppose so," she said.

They walked to the antechamber of the house, and Tilōno opened the outerwear closet. She pulled out her coat and gloves. They were middle class things, but she wouldn't be wearing them in Sīyas' house.

"You're fine after all that happened," Tekīya murmured.

"Of course I am," she said. She considered the Sentinels. Certainly, she would see those in her nightmares. "Maybe not completely. I told Sīyas that I'd come to dinner. She didn't message me to say I could turn this down. Or really at all. I don't know what's going to happen now with the news stories. I'm nervous about those."

Tekīya shook his head and clicked his tongue. "I often forget that you're only eighteen. I've respected you since you were very young. You do good work."

"Thanks."

Her gloved hand rested on the doorknob. Kalðī waited at her feet, ready to be taken out on the lead. "You can walk lim while I'm at dinner. I can come to your stronghold here if you tell me how to get there. You probably won't want to walk the entire time."

"Okay."

She secured the leash and harness around Kalðī, who squirmed with anticipation, and opened the door. The mid-autumn air was chilly, and the sky above had already dissipated from day into star-filled night, clouds on the horizon.

Festival divination had once told her that autumns were hers, that everything good would happen as the sun drove the shadows long, yet before the season faded into winter.

It was a good time to have a success at work and a good season to court a woman for marriage. It was a good thing for the friendship with Tekīya, the bond she couldn't quite put her finger on, a solid connection that had no clear route or path. She *was* only eighteen, and she'd have a lifetime to figure that out. The Hall of Oracles beckoned, and perhaps she would find the answer somewhere in the nābimī books' crisp, typed pages and that scent like sandstone and ink.